Hi . . .

I'm Daizy Star, and I'm in trouble. The kind of trouble that gives you nightmares and threatens to turn your whole life upside-down . . .

I blame my dad! He's gone from being pretty cool to full-on nuts just about overnight . . . and now he's got the worst idea ever. In the history of the universe. And I can't tell anyone about it, not even my best friends . . .

Have you ever told a little white lie and found that it turned into a great big one?

Believe me, it can get kind of complicated . . .

Hugs, happiness and custard doughnuts . . .

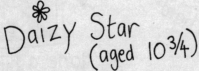

Daizy Star (aged 10¾)

cathy cassidy

Shine On Daizy Star

PUFFIN BOOKS

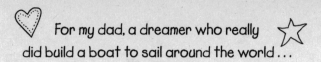

For my dad, a dreamer who really
did build a boat to sail around the world ...

PUFFIN BOOKS

Published by the Penguin Group
Penguin Books Ltd, 80 Strand, London WC2R 0RL, England
Penguin Group (USA) Inc., 375 Hudson Street, New York, New York 10014, USA
Penguin Group (Canada), 90 Eglinton Avenue East, Suite 700, Toronto, Ontario, Canada M4P 2Y3
(a division of Pearson Penguin Canada Inc.)
Penguin Ireland, 25 St Stephen's Green, Dublin 2, Ireland (a division of Penguin Books Ltd)
Penguin Group (Australia), 250 Camberwell Road, Camberwell, Victoria 3124, Australia
(a division of Pearson Australia Group Pty Ltd)
Penguin Books India Pvt Ltd, 11 Community Centre, Panchsheel Park, New Delhi – 110 017, India
Penguin Group (NZ), 67 Apollo Drive, Rosedale, North Shore 0632, New Zealand
(a division of Pearson New Zealand Ltd)
Penguin Books (South Africa) (Pty) Ltd, 24 Sturdee Avenue, Rosebank,
Johannesburg 2196, South Africa

Penguin Books Ltd, Registered Offices: 80 Strand, London WC2R 0RL, England

puffinbooks.com

First published 2009
1

Set in Baskerville MT 13/20pt
Made and printed in England by Clays Ltd, St Ives plc

British Library Cataloguing in Publication Data
A CIP catalogue record for this book is available from the British Library

ISBN: 978–0–141–32519–4

www.greenpenguin.co.uk

Penguin Books is committed to a sustainable future
for our business, our readers and our planet.
The book in your hands is made from paper
certified by the Forest Stewardship Council.

Life is full of surprises – you never know what might be round the corner. Some are good surprises, like when you find a chocolate bar in the bottom of your lunch box, hidden away beneath the cheese and pickle sandwiches. Some are not so good, like when all you find is a shrivelled-up stick of celery.

Unless you happen to love celery, of course, but in my experience nobody does.

Anyhow, life is full of surprises, today especially, because it is the first day of the new school year. We stand around the playground in little clumps, talking too fast, laughing, telling each other what we did in the holidays. Willow went to Cornwall and Beth went to Majorca.

I went to Eastbourne for the day and, of course, it rained. Already the summer is fading, as if it never happened at all.

'Daizy,' Willow whispers, squeezing my arm. 'Have you seen Ethan Miller? Whoa!'

I sneak a look at Ethan, who is playing keepy-uppy with a tennis ball in a corner of the playground while his mates look on. Over the summer holidays, his hair has turned blond and sprouted startling vertical spikes. He is also really, really tanned. In a faintly orange sort of a way.

'I heard he went to Florida in the holidays,' Beth sighs, offering us each a stick of bubblegum. 'He's just soooo cool!'

'Hot, you mean,' Willow corrects her.

If you ask me, Ethan Miller looks like he's been playing with his mum's fake tan, then had some kind of an accident involving a bottle of bleach before finally sticking his fingers into a plug socket.

It's not what I'd call a good look, but Beth and Willow think differently. Their eyes have gone all faraway and dreamy, as if they are looking at a cute little puppy instead of the slouchy, grouchy boy who once dropped a worm down the back of my school sweatshirt back in Year Three.

It's very worrying.

'Be serious,' I say. 'This is Ethan Miller we are talking about.'

'I know,' Willow breathes, as if she has never seen him before. 'I know.'

So that is the first surprise of the day, and it is NOT good. My friends have a crush on the most annoying boy in the school. Scary.

'Are you feeling OK?' I ask Willow. 'You look kind of . . . weird.'

'I feel kind of weird,' she admits. 'Every time Ethan looks at me, my tummy feels like it's full of butterflies.'

'He's not looking at you,' Beth snaps. 'He's looking at me. And butterflies are nothing . . . I feel all feverish and faint. My heart is racing.'

'Perhaps it's some kind of bug?' I ask, and Beth scowls.

'Look, Daizy,' she says. 'We're Year Six, now. We're not little kids any more, we are practically teenagers.'

'We're ten,' I point out.

'Exactly,' she agrees. 'Practically teenagers. We are growing up. Our emotions are in turmoil.'

'They are?'

'They are,' Willow assures me. 'We've got hormones too. I've read about them in your big sister's magazines, Daizy. All those emotions and hormones are boiling away inside of us, like a big vat of school stew.'

'Ewwww,' I say.

Willow and Beth sigh. 'You wouldn't understand,' they say.

They're right – I don't understand why anyone would go all mushy over a boy like Ethan Miller. I decide to take a look at my sister Becca's magazines and find out more about this hormone-stew stuff. I hope it's a temporary thing, because I'm not sure I can cope with a whole year of Beth and Willow acting all lovesick and gooey.

I decide to change the subject. 'I can't believe we are finally in Year Six,' I say. 'Just imagine! We've waited years for this. It's exciting . . . like anything could happen!'

Beth and Willow tear their eyes away from Ethan Miller, grudgingly.

'Are you mad?' Beth asks. 'All that'll happen is we that have to put up with a whole year of Miss Grimwood. Torture!'

That shuts me up.

Miss Grimwood has been teaching Year Six since the time of the dinosaurs. She has iron-grey hair and wears scratchy tweed suits and nylon blouses. Legend has it that she keeps a box of tissues on her desk because when she gets cross, she makes her pupils cry. Even the boys.

Last term, she confiscated Murphy Malone's red studded belt in the middle of the dinner hall, and when he complained that his trousers would fall down without it, she handed him a piece of string instead. Murphy said it was a violation of his human rights, but Miss Grimwood just laughed and dropped the belt in the bin, along with all the leftover chips and cabbage and rice pudding.

I have seen Murphy this morning, and he is wearing cut-off skate shorts, red Converse trainers and a fringy skull-print scarf. I guess he is looking for a showdown with Miss Grimwood, which could be interesting.

The bell rings, and we shuffle into unruly lines along the edge of the playground. I catch sight of my little sister, Pixie, with her shiny shoes and spindly plaits, trailing a skipping rope behind her. She waves, grinning her gap-toothed smile as she lines up with the other Year Two kids.

Mr Smart, the head teacher, stands in front of us. 'Welcome back to Stella Street Primary,' he booms. 'I hope you have all had a wonderful summer – and are ready to do your best in the year ahead!'

We all stand a little straighter, except for Ethan Miller, who just smirks and swaggers and checks that his hair is still vertical.

Mr Smart strides over to our line, narrowing his eyes. 'Year Six, this is your last year of primary,' he says. 'I don't need to tell you how important that is. I want you to make me proud.'

I look along the row of teachers behind him for a glimpse of Miss Grimwood, but I can't see her. Perhaps she is already in Room 12, writing long-division sums on the whiteboard?

'There has been a change to staffing this year,' Mr Smart continues. 'Miss Grimwood is taking a gap year. She is spending the next twelve months running a beach bar on the Costa del Sol.'

I nearly choke on my bubblegum. A half-blown bubble explodes, leaving strands of pink sticky stuff all over my nose.

'A gap year?' Willow blurts. 'Isn't that what students do?'

'A beach bar?' Beth echoes. 'In the Costa del Sol?'

'Miss Grimwood had hidden depths,' Murphy Malone says, impressed. 'Obviously.'

I try to picture her in a leopard-print bikini, sipping cocktails on the beach, but my imagination fails me. I'm kind of glad about that.

'This is your new teacher,' Mr Smart booms. 'Miss Moon . . .'

Beth, Willow and I are wide-eyed. We haven't had a new teacher at Stella Street Primary since . . . well, since forever.

Miss Moon steps forward, grinning. She is young and pretty, with glossy auburn hair, green eyes and a mouth that seems to be smiling all the time. She is wearing dangly earrings and a green tunic dress over pale jeans. None of our other teachers ever wear jeans.

Miss Grimwood taking a gap year in the Costa del Sol . . . that's a surprise. But a new teacher who wears jeans and dangly earrings? That's more of a miracle, really.

'Pleased to meet you, Year Six,' she says, and her voice is soft and kind and clear. 'I think this year is going to be fun!'

Suddenly, I do too.

Room 12 has had a major makeover in the school holidays. The desks are no longer in neat rows but clumped together in groups. A library corner has appeared from nowhere, with rugs, beanbags and a bookcase full of bright, brand-new books.

The shelves above the sink area are stacked with rainbow poster paint, glitter, glue and coloured paper. There are fairy lights draped along the windows, big leafy plants ranged along the sills, and soft, swishy music playing in the background.

Music. In class. Seriously.

'Interesting,' Willow whispers. 'Think she'll let

me play my Ting Tings CD tomorrow?'

We grab a table next to the library corner, and Beth looks around for Ethan Miller, fluttering her lashes. 'There's lots of room here,' she tells him. 'I can help you with your long division . . .'

'I can help you with your spelling, Ethan,' Willow offers. 'Sit next to me!'

I look at my friends in horror. Are they serious?

'Tempting, girls,' Ethan says. 'Tempting. How about you, Daizy? What can you help me with?'

'I can't help you at all,' I snap. 'You're past help. But I'd get my money back on that fake tan, if I were you. You look like you've been rolling around in custard powder, or onion gravy.'

Ethan just laughs. 'You're funny, Daizy Star,' he says, flinging his bag down at a neighbouring table. 'Sorry to disappoint you, girls, but I'm gonna sit with my mates . . . don't want to distract you from your work!'

I breathe a huge sigh of relief, but Beth and Willow are not impressed. 'You could have been a bit friendlier!' Beth says. 'What was all that stuff about onion gravy?'

'Yeah, Daizy!' Willow chips in. 'He might have sat with us!'

'I know,' I say with a shudder.

In the end, Murphy, Tom and Luka slide into the remaining seats. Miss Moon turns off the music and we all snap to attention. 'This is a big year for all of us,' she announces. 'I just know we're going to get along. Why don't we start off by getting to know each other?'

She hands out star-shaped pieces of card, sheets of sparkly paper and pots of glitter, then asks us to draw ourselves in the star-shape. Around the edges, we are supposed to write about our hopes and dreams.

'We all have things that make us special,' Miss Moon explains. 'Skills, hobbies, interests,

character traits. Those are our star qualities, and
they are just as important to me as SATs and the
Literacy Hour. Dreams are special. Don't ever let
them slip through your fingers!'

What if you have more than one dream,
though? Sometimes I want to be a rock star, and
other times I think it'd be cool to be an actress.
Then I change my mind completely and decide
to be a famous artist, living in a crumbling
mansion by the sea, with paint stains on my
fingers and llamas in the garden. It could get very
complicated if you tried to follow every single
dream. One week you'd be miming to rock songs
in front of the mirror or planning your dress for

the red-carpet premiere of your first-ever movie, and the next you'd be painting masterpieces and reading up on how to look after exotic pets.

How are you meant to decide?

Next to me, Willow draws herself singing, with glitter-encrusted notes floating around her picture. Around the edges, she writes about her ambition to be a singer. Beth sketches herself in a sparkly pink tutu, dancing a pirouette. Her ambition is to be a famous ballerina, and then retire to run her own ballet school. I look around.

Murphy draws himself as an artist, Tom as a mad inventor and Luka as a doctor. Ethan, on the next table, is drawing himself as a striker for Man U Football Club.

I pick up a pencil, and draw a round-faced girl with ringletty brown hair, big brown eyes and sparkly hair slides. That's me, Daizy Star.

I like to draw, I like to sing, I like to dance . . .
but I'm not especially good at any of those
things. I'd like to play the guitar, and learn how
juggle and how to do a perfect cartwheel without
ending up in a heap in the corner, but those
things aren't looking likely, either. My
mind is a blank.

Miss Moon pins a huge star-shape snipped
from sparkly gold card on to the wall.

'Every week,' she tells us, 'we will pick out
one special star pupil – our Star of the Week.

Perhaps someone who has worked extra hard, achieved something special or just helped a friend in need . . . I hope, as the year goes on, all of you will have a turn at being Star of the Week. In my class, you will all have your chance to sparkle!'

Miss Moon has the whole class spellbound.

'Cool,' I breathe. Miss Moon starts to pin up our finished pictures, a whole constellation of silver stars clustered around the big gold one. I race to finish mine. I still can't think of my skills and talents, so I add glittery question marks on each point of the star.

I don't know my star quality just yet, but one thing's for sure, I'm going to find it – and when I do, I'm going to shine!

3

I walk home with my little sister, Pixie, talking about Miss Moon and star qualities and dreams. Pixie says her dream is to be a mermaid, with a shimmery green tail and a necklace made from seashells.

'Right,' I say.

I'm not sure if that sort of dream can come true, no matter how hard you work, but I can't tell Pixie that. Six is kind of young to watch your dream crash and burn. Luckily, we have a distraction.

Murphy Malone is leaning against the wall beside the bakery, with a bag of doughnuts and a smile.

Murphy Malone is my best boy mate – he lives across the road from us in Silver Street. Murphy wants to be a fashion designer when he's older, and he is always trying out new looks. He wears cool clothes and has interesting haircuts and listens to strange-sounding bands on his iPod.

'Hey,' he says now, falling into step beside us. 'I have custard doughnuts . . . want to share?'

Murphy has an obsession with custard doughnuts, but I'm not complaining. Pixie takes one and shows Murphy the model she made in school, which is large and lumpy and involves loo-roll tubes, lots of masking tape and a few strips of soggy papier mâché. 'Nice,' he tells her. 'Very artistic.'

'Thank you. It's a three-headed dinosaur,' she says.

'Ah,' Murphy says wisely. 'They're extinct.'

Pixie looks crestfallen. 'Are you sure about that?' she asks.

'Well,' he considers. 'I've never seen one, but I suppose nobody knows for sure . . .'

We cut across the park, sharing the doughnuts and taking turns to play on the tyre swing. Murphy hangs upside down so that his long fringe brushes the ground, which makes Pixie laugh.

He is on a high because Miss Moon did not throw his skull-print scarf into the bin. In fact, she said it was very stylish, but perhaps a bit warm for September. Murphy told her that he was willing to suffer for the sake of looking good, and she just laughed.

'At last!' Murphy says. 'A teacher who understands that school uniform can be creative and exciting! Miss Moon is the best teacher ever!'

I think maybe she is.

Back home at Silver Street, my big sister, Becca, has abandoned her maths homework to make potato salad, and there's a quiche warming in the oven.

If Becca has a star quality, it is probably school work. She is the kind of girl who is always up to date with her homework. She plays the flute and wears perfect school uniform and reads revision guides for fun, even in the holidays – she wants to be a teacher, just like Dad.

Next to Becca, I am clumsy and chaotic, like a disaster waiting to happen, but my big sister never makes me feel bad. She loves me anyway, and I love her, and both of us adore Pixie, even if she does still believe in mermaids and three-headed dinosaurs.

'I was going to make fairy cakes, to celebrate our first day back at school,' Becca says. 'But I could only find muesli and dried prunes in the cupboard, so I thought I'd better not.'

Pixie and I spread a cloth across the garden table so we can eat outside, picnic style. Pixie places the three-headed dinosaur in the middle of the table, with a flower in its mouth for decoration. Well, one of its mouths, anyway.

I pick up one of Becca's *TeenGal* magazines from the coffee table and flick through, looking for clues on why Beth and Willow have gone all mushy over Ethan Miller. It doesn't mention hormones, but there's lots of stuff about hairstyles and lipstick and flirting with boys. Is this really what being a teenager is all about? It sounds slightly depressing.

Then Dad arrives, his bicycle skidding across the gravel drive. A bottle of wine is poking out from the top of his rucksack, and a carrier bag from the bakery dangles from the bike's handlebars.

Dad is a geography teacher at Green Lane Community School, and he cycles to work because he's kind of obsessive about the environment. He says it keeps him fit and keeps a lid on the stress, but I'm not sure if that's worked today. He has a strange, wild-eyed look about him. His tie has gone askew in the breeze and thrown itself over one shoulder, and is hanging down behind.

'Everything OK, Dad?' I ask.

'Never better!' He grins, but the grin is too bright. It's the way I look when I'm about to go in to see the dentist, but don't want anyone to know how nervous I'm feeling. Dad strides through to the garden and surveys our picnic table.

'Fantastic idea,' he says. 'Today is a day to celebrate!'

'Exactly,' Becca says, looking up from her maths homework. 'First day back at school and all that.'

Dad just laughs, a strange, unsettling laugh, and dumps the bottle of wine and the carrier bag down on the table. Inside it is a box containing a huge, iced cake.

Something very strange is going on. I lift the

cake out on to a plate.
It is a carrot cake, but not
the loaf-shaped, stodgy
kind Dad sometimes
makes. This one is topped
with buttercream with an icing-sugar carrot on
the top. It makes my mouth water.

By the time Mum's car pulls into the drive,
Dad has showered and changed and slipped his
favourite CD into the player. 'Good day at work,
Livvi?' he asks.

Mum is a nurse at the big hospital in town.
She is always full of stories about the people on
the wards, like the sweet old lady who wears a
purple wig, the man with the red pyjamas who
sings sad ballads in the middle of the night, and
the fitness instructor with a broken leg who has a
secret stash of Twix bars hidden under his bed.

Sometimes, though, there aren't any stories
and Mum is tired and stressy and sad. I suppose
that looking after people who aren't well must be
hard work.

'I had a good day,' Mum replies. 'You?'

'The best!' Dad laughs again, and it makes me nervous.

'Kids? How was school?'

'Great,' says Becca. 'I signed up for orchestra and advanced maths again, and I might even get to be form captain!'

'My day was good too,' I say. 'We've got this great new teacher, Miss Moon . . .'

'I made a dinosaur out of papier mâché,' Pixie chips in. 'It's got three heads!'

'Ah,' Mum says politely, eyeing the cardboard creature dripping glue quietly on to the tablecloth. 'Fabulous, Pixie!'

We sit down to eat, and the late-afternoon sun warms our backs and the smell of jasmine wafts down from the trellis, and it's all just about perfect. Except that today is a day of surprises, and the biggest one of all is yet to come.

'I'm impressed, Mike,' Mum says, sipping her wine. 'Wine and cake? You really did have a good day at work, didn't you? I know you weren't looking forward to going back, but I told you it'd be fine, didn't I?'

Dad's smile is so wide it looks like it's fraying around the edges. Can't Mum see that something is wrong?

'Livvi . . .' He takes a deep breath. 'I've quit my job.'

As surprises go, it's more of a bombshell.

Mum chokes on her wine, spattering the tablecloth. Pixie has to pat her on the back.

Dad sighs. 'I haven't been enjoying work lately, as you know. I'm trying my best to teach those kids about the hole in the ozone layer and the melting polar icecap, but all they care about

25

whether they have enough cash to buy a Big Mac after school. And . . . well, there was a small incident.'

'Incident?' Mum echoes.

'This afternoon, I was teaching the Year Nines about global warming. You know that big map of the world I've got on the wall? Craig Kennedy struck a match and set fire to it,' Dad says. 'I had to put it out with the fire extinguisher, but of course, the fire alarms had gone off by then. The whole school had to be evacuated.'

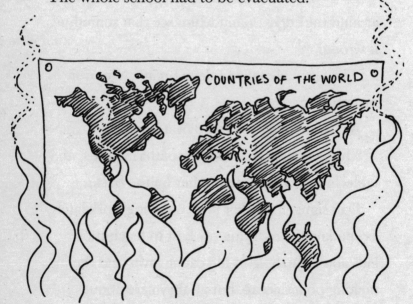

Mum hides behind her hands, Becca's eyes widen in horror and Pixie stifles a giggle and has to stuff a slice of quiche into her mouth to muffle the sound. Me, I just feel bad for Dad.

'When all the fuss had died down, I asked Craig why he did it. He said he'd always wanted to set the world on fire,' Dad goes on. 'You see what I'm dealing with? Well, this was the last straw.

'I told the Head I'd had enough. He said he'd be very sorry to see me go, but that perhaps a break would help me find my love of teaching again. I don't even have to work out my notice . . . they have enough people to cover until a new teacher is appointed.'

'Oh, Mike,' Mum says. 'What have you done?'

I put my hand out across the table to Dad, and he takes it and squeezes it tight, winking at me.

'You can get another job,' Becca says. 'You'll have to, really.'

'I don't want one,' Dad says firmly. 'This is not a disaster – it's a chance to jump off the treadmill

27

and do something new. For years now, I've felt like a hamster in a cage, running faster and faster on my wheel and getting nowhere at all. It's time to break free. If I don't, I'll end up a sad, shrivelled-up old has-been, with nothing left but regrets and broken dreams.'

I swallow hard. I don't want my dad to be a sad, shrivelled-up old has-been.

'We can try the things we've always wanted to,' Dad is saying. 'Live life to the full! I've been thinking about this all summer, wishing we could have the chance to follow our dreams . . .'

'This isn't a dream, it's a nightmare,' Mum says.

Dad laughs. 'I know it's a shock, but trust me, it's the best thing that's ever happened to us. It's a second chance. I've given this a lot of thought, and I have a plan . . .'

'Plan?' Mum repeats. 'What plan?'

Dad drains his wine glass and grins at us each in turn.

'We're going to sail around the world,' he says.

I think if there are any more surprises like this one lurking in the shadows, I will go to my room, curl up under my duvet and stay there forever. Or longer, maybe.

The place is like a war zone.

Mum is yelling at Dad. Dad is yelling back, telling Mum to stop being such a scaredy-cat and to grab life with both hands before it's too late. Becca says there is no way she is going to mess up her studies just because Dad let his Year Nine class set fire to the school, and Pixie just asks if we should start packing yet, and if so, will there be room for her three-headed dinosaur?

'Are you having a mid-life crisis?' Becca asks.

'You've been acting weird ever since you turned forty, like you've just woken up and discovered that life is passing you by. You're not a kid any more – you're a middle-aged teacher with a receding hairline.'

'All right,' Dad says. 'Don't rub it in.'

'She's got a point,' Mum says. 'It's quite common. Middle-aged blokes wanting to make their mark on the world before it's too late.'

'Stacey's dad had a mid-life crisis,' Becca continues. 'He bought a motorbike and started wearing leather trousers. Yuck. But couldn't you just try that if you want to do something stupid? Because there is just no way I am sailing around the world!'

'I don't want leather trousers,' Dad says. 'I want to build a boat!'

'Build a boat?' Mum snorts. 'You can't even put together a flat-pack bookshelf! Mike, get real!'

Dad sighs. 'It's my dream, Livvi. It was your dream too.'

This is news to me. I thought my mum dreamt about piles of neatly ironed washing and freshly hoovered carpets. 'My dream is to have a nice, peaceful, ordinary life,' Mum huffs.

See? I was nearly right.

'Mine is to stay on dry land, and be form captain, and have a dad who isn't trying to wreck everything,' Becca adds.

'Mine is to be a mermaid,' Pixie says.

'Yeah, right,' Becca snaps. 'There's no such thing as mermaids.'

'There is so!'

Pixie starts to cry, and Mum puts one arm around her and one around Becca. 'Now see what you've done?' she asks Dad.

Dad looks at me. 'What do you think, Daizy?' he asks, and somehow I don't think he's asking about mermaids.

I think that my dad has finally flipped.

I remember when Dad was cool and popular, the kind of teacher who organized end-of-term trips to Alton Towers and often came home with wonky jam tarts or whatever the kids had been making in their home ec. lessons that week. Then he got all fired up about saving the environment, and his sense of humour fizzled away. This year the class trip was to an organic farm, so the kids could learn how to build the perfect compost heap and make nettle soup. That was never really going to compare with Alton Towers, was it?

I know the shine has gone from teaching for Dad, but ditching your job to sail around the world is kind of drastic. OK, maybe he'd like to travel a bit, see the places he teaches about . . . sail past the Statue of Liberty at sunset, or moor up on a beach in Zanzibar. I'd like to see the world too – I just don't want

to see it from the deck of a boat. I don't like boats, and I really hate the water. I went on a pedalo at Center Parcs once, and even that made me seasick.

'What about school?' I ask in a small voice.

'School?' Dad scoffs. 'We'll take you out of school for a year. Sailing around the world will be the best education ever!'

Becca looks horrified.

I look at Dad's face, all sparkly and bright and full of excitement. I know his idea is a bad one. A very bad one. The problem is, it's his dream. Only today, Miss Moon was telling the class that you should never let a dream slip through your fingers.

I do not want to sail around the world in a home-made boat, but I am not going to be the one to trample all over Dad's dream.

'I'll come with you,' I say bravely.

Dad grins. 'That's my girl!' he says. 'I knew you would, Daizy! I'll be the Captain and you can be First Mate.'

'I'll come too,' Pixie pipes up. 'Can I be First Mermaid?'

'Whatever you like, Pixie!' Dad grins.

Mum sighs heavily. 'Don't tell me,' she says. 'I'm Galley Slave and Ship's Medical Officer rolled into one, right?'

Becca looks at us, eyes wide. 'Are you crazy?' she asks. 'Dad walks out on his job and decides to sail around the world, and you all go along with it like he's suggested a day at the seaside?'

Dad just shrugs. 'Sometimes the craziest ideas are the best ones,' he says. 'Give it a go, Becca. You'll enjoy it, I know you will!'

'It's not happening,' Becca says. 'Mum, tell him!'

Mum frowns. 'I'm not saying we should do it,' she says haltingly. 'But perhaps we should think about it? It's something your dad and I used to talk about, years ago, before you girls were born.'

Becca gathers up her maths homework, lips trembling, her carrot cake untouched. One

perfect tear rolls down her cheek. I haven't seen
my big sister cry since the time she came last in
the inter-schools spelling tournament four years
ago, and even then it didn't really count because
it turned out that she was coming down with
chicken pox.

My big sister does not cry . . . usually.

Becca sniffs, and her eyes well with tears again.
'My life is over,' she says.

5

I can't sleep. A million things are running through my mind, and they're not nice things. Pixie's half-packed suitcase, Becca crying, Mum yelling, Dad's hopeful grin as he told us about his big dream . . . the one that turned out to be everyone else's nightmare.

It's the worst idea I have ever heard. Sailing around the world? It'd be like that film *Titanic*, all icebergs and life jackets and crashing waves, only the boat would be smaller and scabbier and made from splintered old planks, most likely. Why now, when I am just about to start Year Six? Why now, when I have fab friends and the best teacher in the universe? I might never find my star quality, floating around in the middle of the Atlantic Ocean.

At school I don't mention Dad's plan to sail around the world to anyone. If I talk about it, it might start to feel real, and that's something I'm not ready for right now.

No, it's safer to fix a smile on my face and pretend that nothing is wrong. At least at school I can pretend that nothing scary is happening – or nothing involving boats, anyhow. Beth and Willow are a different kind of scary.

'I think I'm in love with Ethan Miller,' Beth sighs at lunchtime.

'I liked him before you!' Willow protests. 'Since Year Three.'

'What, when you called him a horrible pig with a face like a squashed football?' Beth recalls, raising an eyebrow. 'Yeah, right.'

'I may have said that, but I meant it in a good way!'

I can see a fall-out brewing, so I wade in, ready to smooth things out. 'Don't fight over Ethan,' I tell them. 'He's not worth it!'

The two of them turn on me.

'He is totally worth it!' Beth insists.

'You don't get it, Daizy, do you?' Willow says pityingly. 'Ethan's good looks and animal magnetism have no effect on you at all. You'll understand one day, when you're a bit more grown up.'

'I'm very grown up!' I protest, outraged. 'I just have taste!'

They shake their heads sadly, as if they know something I don't, which leaves me feeling all frowny and cross. Ethan Miller has a lot to answer for.

When the bell rings to signal the end of lunchtime, we troop inside to find sheets of sugar paper and a selection of paints, pastels and inks on each desk. Art!

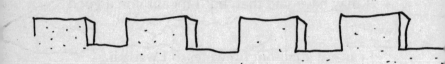

'Hush, now, class,' Miss Moon says as we settle down. 'I have exciting news. Mr Smart wants to create an adventure playground for the little ones this year – and he wants to consult you, the Year Six pupils. After all, you know more about this school than anyone – and you also remember what it was like when you were younger.'

'There wasn't much to do, back then,' Freya Jenks recalls. 'An adventure playground would be great!'

'I think so,' Miss Moon agrees. 'And it would be a way for you to leave a lasting impression on Stella Street Primary. Mr Smart wants a design that is creative, challenging and fun.

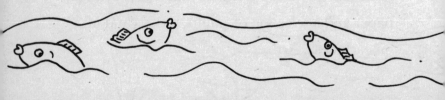

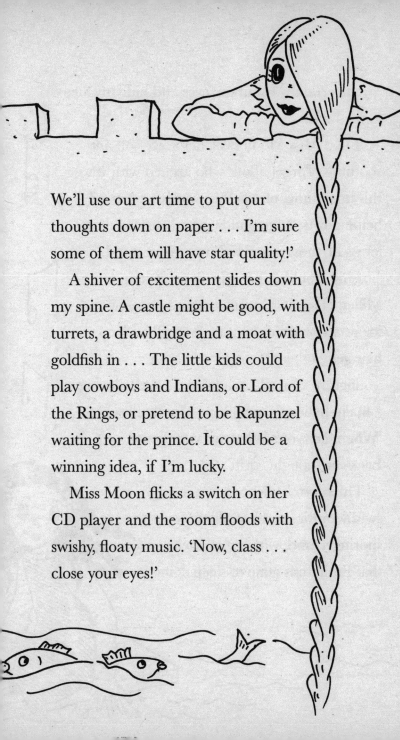

We'll use our art time to put our thoughts down on paper . . . I'm sure some of them will have star quality!'

A shiver of excitement slides down my spine. A castle might be good, with turrets, a drawbridge and a moat with goldfish in . . . The little kids could play cowboys and Indians, or Lord of the Rings, or pretend to be Rapunzel waiting for the prince. It could be a winning idea, if I'm lucky.

Miss Moon flicks a switch on her CD player and the room floods with swishy, floaty music. 'Now, class . . . close your eyes!'

Uncertainly, I shut my eyes and hide my face in my hands.

'OK,' Miss Moon says, her voice soft and soothing. 'Forget about who argued with who this lunchtime, or whether you got a second helping of sponge pudding and custard . . . let go of those worries. Empty your mind.'

This shouldn't be difficult for Ethan Miller. His mind is usually empty, except for occasional thoughts of football and hair gel.

'Picture yourself as a five-year-old, playing a make-believe game,' Miss Moon tells us. 'Where are you? What are you doing? Let your thoughts drift . . .'

The room is silent except for the swishy music, and a snuffling, snoring sound, which may mean that Ethan has gone to sleep.

I try to imagine castles and unicorns, but instead I see turquoise water, glinting silver in the sun. I am on a raft, floating towards a golden sunset, my hand trailing through warm waves.

'Let your imagination run wild!'

The light fades, and I shiver a little. The sea is darker now, rougher. The raft has become the deck of a huge, rolling ship, and I grip its wheel, wearing orange waterproof trousers. I can feel the steady drip, drip, drip of icy rain down my neck.

 Then I see it – a ship
whose sails hang in
grey tatters, whose crew
laugh as they raise the pirate
flag and plough right across
our bows. There's a crunch of splintering wood
and a bloodthirsty yell as the pirates swing
aboard, swords shining in the moonlight . . .

'OK, class,' Miss Moon says. 'Hold that
thought. Open your eyes and use the art
materials to capture the dream and turn it into
a design for our adventure playground!'

I pick up a pastel and start to work, using
quick, vivid strokes, until my hands are streaked
with black and blue and green.

'OK,' Miss Moon says after a while. 'Let's
see what you've come up with.'

I sit back and look around me, as if coming
out of a trance. Then I take a long, hard look at
my drawing, and my heart sinks. I have messed
up, majorly. Again.

Miss Moon collects up the work. I don't want

to hand mine over, but there is no escape. 'Interesting,' she says, and begins pinning the pictures to the wall so we can discuss them.

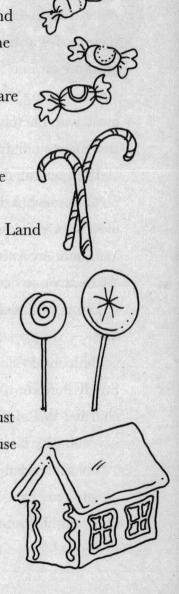

The designs are cool. There are a few versions of the castle idea I'd been planning – Murphy's even has the drawbridge and the flag, but not the moat full of goldfish. Beth's sketch is like the Land of Sweets from that ballet her dance class put on last Christmas, all candy canes and lollipop trees and a gingerbread playhouse with an icing-sugar roof. I'd have loved that, back when I was five. Even Ethan must have woken up in the end because he has painted a huge football-shaped climbing frame.

The one that stands out the most, though . . . is mine.

On a pinboard filled with cute, kidsy designs, mine is dark, dangerous and downright scary. I have drawn a shipwrecked boat, with dark waves crashing around it. Pirates are swinging on to the wreck, waving their swords about. I got so carried away with the daydream that I forgot we were designing a children's adventure playground.

I've spent all day trying to forget what's going on at home, but the nightmares won't go away, even in broad daylight.

'There are some great ideas,' Miss Moon says. 'Does any one design stand out?'

Ethan Miller clears his throat. 'Daizy's,' he says.

Beth and Willow shoot me envious looks. Surely they know I am immune to Ethan's charms? Well, I would be, if he had any. I will never forgive him for the worm incident.

I blush scarlet, from the tips of my ears right down to my toes. 'I got a bit carried away,' I blurt out. 'I forgot what we were supposed to be doing . . .'

Miss Moon nods. 'It's a little rough around the edges, but Daizy's daydream is so vivid we can all see it too!'

'But . . . I didn't design anything!' I argue.

'No, you didn't,' Miss Moon agrees.
'But the idea is good.'

'A pirate theme,' Beth says thoughtfully.
'That'd be cool. Kids could play on the

shipwreck . . . We could put a pirate flag on the mast, with rope ladders and scramble nets leading up to the deck . . .'

'And a plank to walk, landing in a sandpit!' Willow suggests.

'We could have that rubbery safety-stuff you get in playgrounds all around it,' Murphy chips in. 'In blue, with sharks painted on, and stepping stones. If anyone strays, they get eaten by sharks . . .'

'We could have a treasure chest inside the cabin, filled with jewels and dressing-up stuff!' Freya says.

I just sit there, my eyes open wide, my mouth a perfect 'o' of surprise. They can see all that in one murky picture?

'Let's make a shortlist,' Miss Moon says. 'Vote for our favourite ideas, so that we can show them to Mr Smart, and to the little ones.'

So we vote. Murphy's castle gets seven votes, Beth's Land of Sweets gets five and Ethan's climbing frame gets three, but a whopping

TWELVE people vote for my pirate idea.

I start drawing it out again, properly this time, showing the scramble nets, the treasure chest, the plank and the sandpit.

Supposing Mr Smart likes my idea too? Supposing the infant-class kids agree, and they go ahead and build it right out there on the infants' playground? That would be kind of scary, but amazing too.

Of course, by then it'll be too late. I'll be halfway across the Atlantic Ocean, wearing orange waterproof trousers, in the middle of my very own nightmare.

I hold my breath for days. Not literally – if I did that, I'd turn purple and keel over, gasping, but you know what I mean. I just want to find out what Mr Smart and the infant kids think about my idea. OK, it was an accidental idea, but still, some of the best inventions in the world happen like that, don't they?

If my idea gets chosen, it could prove I have star quality – if not for designing, then for daydreaming at the very least.

My nightmares are top-quality.

Last week Luka Kinski was Star of the Week,

because he got twenty out of twenty on every maths and spelling test all week long. Of course, that just made everyone study a little bit harder. This week, though, it has nothing to do with test results. It's Tasha Graham, because she picked up a Coke can Ethan had dropped in the school playground and put it in the bin. Ethan got a telling-off and Tasha got to be a star, and now everybody is being extra careful about not dropping litter, or picking it up if they see any.

Next week, Star of the Week could be something different again. Next week, if I'm lucky, it could be me.

My little sister, Pixie, has star quality, that's for sure. She was born with webbed feet. OK, they're not actually webbed, but they may as well be – she's amazing at swimming. Pixie goes to a club called Little Seals every Thursday, and she's just about the best in the class.

I take Pixie over to the leisure centre straight after school, and Murphy Malone tags along. We sit in the gallery, eating ice lollies and watching as Pixie splashes about below.

'She's good,' Murphy says. 'Amazingly good, for a six-year-old.'

'Amazingly,' I sigh.

'She's a natural,' Murphy says.

'She is,' I agree.

'It's like she has no fear of water at all –'

'All right, you don't have to go on about it!' I snap.

Murphy looks startled. 'I didn't mean anything!' he protests.

Murphy probably didn't mean anything, but swimming is a bit of a sore point with me. Pixie is the swim-star, but my whole family love the water – all except me.

I hate it. I hate the big, bright clinical look of the swimming pool, the smell of the chlorine in the turquoise water, the sting of it in your eyes, the lukewarm, chemical taste of it when you swallow a mouthful or inhale it by mistake. I hate the way the bottom of the pool gives way beneath your feet, so that one minute you're balancing on one leg on the scratchy blue tiles and the next you're scrabbling and squirming and going under.

It wasn't always like that. I was quite happy in the water when I was little, but everything changed one awful day when I was four. We were at the pool, Mum, Dad, me, Becca and Pixie – Pixie was just a baby, all trussed up in a special swim-nappy and one of those rubber rings you sit in as you splash about.

I was wearing one of Becca's old swimsuits. It was bright pink with a frill around the hips, and I thought it was the coolest thing ever. There was just one problem – it had a hole in it, from where Becca had snagged it on a rose bush in the garden, and the hole was at the back . . . right on the bum. Mum had stitched over the hole with pink wool, but it wasn't quite the right shade of pink and if you looked carefully, you could see the repair.

'Nobody will notice,' Mum had told me. 'Not once you get into the water!'

As I walked out of the changing room that day, I kept looking down over my left shoulder, peering at the pink stitching. To me, it looked huge. Everybody would be able to see it, surely? Then I remembered what Mum had said. I let go of Becca's hand, sprinted for the edge of the pool and jumped in. I didn't know it was the deep end, did I?

I sank like a stone, swallowed half the pool and had to be hauled out by Dad while half the sports centre looked on. You can bet they all got a really good view of the patched-up hole in my swimsuit bum too.

It was the scariest thing ever – and I still hate swimming. You don't get over that kind of thing in a hurry.

I dread it when we have swimming lessons with the school – Murphy and Willow and Beth are always in the top group, while I'm stuck in the shallow end with armbands and a float like some little kid, even though I'm almost eleven years old.

Last time we had lessons, I faked a three-week-long cold, but Dad got wise to me and stopped writing the notes. 'You have to face your fear,' he told me. 'Keep trying! We'll get you swimming, don't worry!'

'Sorry,' Murphy says, now. 'I didn't think, Daizy. '

'I know,' I tell him. 'I'm sorry I snapped at you. It's just . . . well, it's hard to have a little sister who swims like a fish, when you swim like . . . like . . .'

'A brick?' Murphy suggests helpfully.

I crack a smile. 'Don't push your luck,' I tell

him. 'I have other talents. I'm just not sure what they are, exactly . . .'

I wait for Murphy to jump in and tell me what my talents are, but he just shrugs and smiles, which is a bit worrying.

Down in the pool, the Little Seals are climbing out of the water, heading for the changing rooms. Pixie looks up, catches my eye and waves.

'Murphy,' I ask carefully, as we watch the kids tiptoe away to the changing rooms. 'What would you say my star qualities are? What am I really, really good at?'

Murphy frowns. 'Well,' he considers, 'you always have lots of crazy ideas . . .'

'That's not a star quality,' I scoff. 'Be serious.'

'OK,' Murphy says. 'Your talents are . . . you're very good at . . . well, lots of things, but you're especially brilliant at . . . um . . .'

'Yes?'

Murphy is chewing his lip.

'Murphy?' I ask him gently. 'I'm especially brilliant at . . . what?'

'Being you!' he announces.

That's not quite what I was hoping for. Isn't everyone good at being themselves? My shoulders slump.

'C'mon, Daizy,' he says. 'You're cool, kind, caring . . . and loads of fun too. You're the one and only Daizy Star! And Miss Moon is right – you can do anything you set your mind to!'

'You think so?' I ask.

'I know so. Race you down the stairs!'

He legs it down into the lobby, all flailing elbows and floppy fringe, and I race after – I almost catch him too. Pixie is waiting, with damp hair and a mile-wide smile.

'Was I good, Daizy?' she wants to know.

'Better than good,' I tell her. 'The best.'

'Dad!' Pixie yells suddenly. And sure enough,

Dad appears, pink-faced from cycling, striding towards us with a sheet of paper in his hand.

'Dad!' I echo. 'I didn't know you'd be here!'

'I thought I'd see how my best girls are doing,' he replies. 'Make the most of my new-found leisure.'

'Leisure?' Murphy asks, looking at me.

My heart sinks to the bottom of my Converse trainers. I haven't told anyone about the flaming map and the lesson on global warming, obviously. I haven't told anyone that Dad has jacked his job in to build a boat and sail around the world, because if I say it out loud it'll be real, and I just don't want it to be. I need a bit more time to get used to the idea myself before I unleash it on the world.

'Dad's got a few days off,' I say quietly, before he gets a chance to tell Murphy the whole story, but Dad isn't even listening.

He hands me the sheet of paper.

'Look at this, Daizy!' he says.

I read the flyer with a feeling of doom.

The Baby Dolphin Club are running swimming classes for beginners twice a week, just after school. Success is guaranteed.

'I've signed you up,' Dad says brightly. 'You'll soon be swimming!'

'Dad, no!' I argue. 'You know how I feel about swimming . . .'

'It's important,' Dad says.

'Very important,' Pixie agrees. 'Especially now that we're –'

'I'll do it!' I blurt, before Dad and Pixie can blab everything to Murphy and ruin any last shreds of normality my life may have. 'I'll join this class, learn to swim, OK?'

Murphy gives me a sympathetic grin. 'You can do it, Daizy Star,' he grins.

'Remember? You can do anything you set your mind to.'

I smile weakly. Just what have I got myself into?

Murphy slopes off down the steps with a wave and a grin. I breathe a sigh of relief. My secret is safe – for now, at least.

7

You wouldn't think that things could get worse, but of course, they can. My sister Becca, who has been flumping about for the past few days looking huffy and tragic, comes out of the bathroom on Friday morning in neon-pink eyeshadow with thick smudges of black eyeliner under each eye. Her hair is wild, back-combed and topped with a black lace ribbon. She looks like an extra from *The Addams Family*.

'Are you in fancy dress?' I ask, before she can sneak back into her room. 'Is it a non-uniform day? Raising money for . . . I don't know, deprived teen goths or something?'

'Funny,' Becca says. 'It's my new look. What d'you think?'

'Scary,' I say. 'I'm not sure about the pink eyeshadow, or the eyeliner. You look like you've been up all night crying.'

'I like it,' Becca sniffs. 'So what if I look sad and scary? That's how I feel – and angry too! Dad is ruining my life. All those years I worked hard at school, wore perfect uniform . . . Where did it get me? Nowhere!'

'But . . .'

'But nothing, Daizy,' she says. 'I'm going to have some fun while I still can. What's wrong with that?'

Becca picks up her rucksack and puts on her iPod. It's so loud I can hear the crashing, wailing rackety music right across the landing.

'Love ya, Daizy,' she says, then runs down the stairs and out of the front door before Mum or Dad can catch her.

At least at school I can still try to ignore the fact that my family are going crazy. I do not have to think about sailing around the world or swimming lessons with the Baby Dolphin Club, or a sister who has gone from goody-two-shoes to goth in less than four days.

At least Murphy hasn't asked any awkward questions about Dad's time off or the sudden importance of swimming lessons. Phew. I just have to listen to Beth and Willow getting mushy over Ethan Miller and finish off my new-look playground design and figure out the mysteries of the decimal point. It's practically a holiday.

But then I go home, and I can't escape the

nightmare. Dad has enrolled in a woodwork-skills class and started to buy hammers, saws and pots of stinky glue. Thick, dusty books on sailing are piled around the room, and navigation charts are spread out across the dining table.

Mum is trying to clear a space for the tea, but it's a losing battle. Dad doesn't even notice – he is combing the Internet for information on kit boats.

'Our boat must be stable enough to withstand an ocean storm,' he tells us. 'It needs to be sturdy and strong and hard to capsize . . .'

I have a sudden vision of us floundering around in icy seas, clinging on to splintered bits of wreckage. I swallow hard. There are so many things to think of: icebergs, tropical storms, whales, leaks, gale-force winds, pirates . . .

'There's a kit here that seems really good value,' Dad goes on. 'They send you all the pieces, ready cut, with plans and instructions. It's foolproof.'

'It will need to be,' Mum says darkly.

'I'm going to order it,' Dad says. 'The *Haddock*, it's called.'

I stifle a snort. 'The *Haddock*? Seriously?'

'Isn't that a fish?' Pixie wants to know.

'It is. It's a good name for a steady, sensible, ocean-going boat,' Dad says. 'I don't see what's funny.'

'Nor do I,' Mum says, hiding a smirk. 'It tastes very nice fried and battered and served with chips too.'

'Oh, for goodness' sake!'

Becca appears in the doorway wearing purple lipstick and black nail varnish, with her hair carefully crimped and back-combed. She is wearing a black tutu, red fishnet tights over black leggings and clumpy biker boots with shiny silver buckles.

Dad glances up from the laptop and almost falls off his chair.

'Rebecca Star, what on earth are you wearing?' he chokes out.

'Honestly,' Becca says. 'Everyone wears stuff like this, these days. It's the fashion.' She winks at me cheekily.

'Are you going out?' Mum asks carefully. Becca hardly ever goes out, unless it's to orchestra practice or advanced-maths lessons, but I don't think she's all dressed up for a night in with her homework.

'No big deal,' Becca says, rolling her eyes. 'I'm going to the park with Skidd and Razz and Ziggy.'

'Skidd and . . . what? Who are these people?' Dad blurts. 'I don't like the sound of them!'

'They're my friends,' Becca says.

They are, actually. I happen to know that Skidd is Sophie Skidmore, Razz is Rachel Lowe and Ziggy is Maria Zigowski. They've been Becca's friends since nursery school, but Dad doesn't know this. He looks terrified. He is probably imagining black-clad teenagers with leather jackets and chains hanging from their trousers.

Actually, it's a while since I last saw Skidd, Razz and Ziggy. Dad may not be too far off the mark.

'I'll be back by ten,' Becca says. 'Not that you care.'

'Of course I care!' Dad yells, but Becca has gone, in a blur of hairspray and black net, slamming the door behind her. 'What's going on?' Dad asks. 'Where did she get those clothes from? That attitude?'

'It's just a phase,' Mum says soothingly. 'She's rebelling, that's all. It's a teenage thing.'

I wonder if Dad wanting to sail around the world is a phase too. I hope so.

'This going out on a school night will have to stop,' Dad says grimly. 'Becca has her grades to think of. She's getting in with the wrong sort of crowd . . . thank goodness we're leaving all this behind. I will not stand by and let Becca turn into a juvenile delinquent!'

'I don't think it's got to that stage just yet,' Mum sighs. 'Go back to your boat kits.'

'Am I a juvenile delinquent?' Pixie pipes up. 'I am almost seven. What is one, anyway?'

'A juvenile delinquent is a young person who is very, very naughty,' Mum says. 'You're definitely not one, Pixie, and nor is Becca.'

'Well, I'm not really young any more, am I?' Pixie says thoughtfully. 'After all, I will be seven next month.'

'Exactly,' Dad says absently.

Pixie looks as though she might explode. 'I'm actually very grown up,' she says. 'Because I am very nearly, almost, just about SEVEN!'

'Dad,' I say, hiding a smile. 'I think Pixie's trying to tell you something!'

He tears his eyes away from the laptop. 'Sorry, Pixie,' he says. 'Almost seven years old! How about that?'

'So can I have a mermaid party, with all my friends?'

Mum looks up from her battle with the navigation charts. 'Oh, sweetheart, this might not be a good year for a party . . .'

I can see what she means. Planks of golden yellow pine and random coils of thick rope have invaded our living room. Boxes of nails and screws swarm across the carpet, and a vast roll of unbleached canvas lies slumped in a corner, like a beached whale.

It's like living in a shipyard.

'Next year then?' Pixie pleads.

But by next year, we could be aboard the
Haddock, adrift in the Pacific Ocean or lurching
through a tropical storm. We could be anywhere
at all. Mermaid parties will not be an option.

Pixie's shoulders slump. 'OK,' she says. 'Never
mind.'

Later, when my little sister has gone to bed,
Mum says she thinks that Pixie should have her
party, no matter how awkward it might be.

'She never complains,' Mum reminds us. 'She
always looks on the bright side. I don't suppose
she wants to leave her friends any more than the

rest of us do, but does she moan? No. She deserves her mermaid party!'

'Totally,' I nod. 'We can make her a cake – mermaid-shaped! And maybe I can make her a mermaid's tail, so she can dress up and look the part . . . it could be her present!'

'Fantastic idea, Daizy,' Mum says. 'Mike, what do you think?'

'OK,' Dad agrees. 'We'll give Pixie her party. I suppose I can tidy the boat-building stuff away, just for one afternoon.'

'We don't even have to have the party here,' Mum points out. 'That would make it all much simpler. After all, she wants a mermaid party, doesn't she? And she's a real water-baby, obviously. What better place . . .'

I stop listening then, because I can see where this is going. A girl who loves to swim? A mermaid-themed party? There is only one sensible place to hold a party like that.

Why do these things always happen to me? Why?

Mum rings the leisure centre and arranges to hire part of the swimming pool for Pixie's seventh birthday party.

Whoop-de-doo.

8

I wish I was a million miles away . . . but not on a flat-pack boat, sailing around the world, obviously. It's just that I don't want to be right here, right now. The smell of chlorine is sharp in my nostrils as I pull on my swimsuit and wriggle into orange armbands and two rubber rings. It may look a bit odd, but I am not taking any chances.

I am stuffing my clothes into a locker when a small boy in polka dot swim shorts pokes me on the arm. He is not the cutest kid I have ever seen – he looks like a frog, with bulging eyes and wet lips and a slimy kind of look about him.

'What are you wearing all those for?' he asks.

'I'm learning to swim,' I say politely. 'With the Baby Dolphins.'

'Armbands and rubber rings aren't allowed,' he sneers. 'How come you're in the Baby Dolphin class, anyway? How old are you?'

'Much older than you,' I huff. 'I'm practically a teenager!'

'No, you're not,' Frog Boy smirks. 'My sister is a teenager, and she wears a bra!'

I should slam the locker door and walk away, I know. When you meet the lowlifes of this world, the slimy green creatures who have just crawled out from under a stone, the best thing to do is blank them. That way, they might just crawl back to where they came from, and leave you alone.

Sadly, I do not walk away. I fold my arms across my chest and glare at the slimy little creep.

'I wear a bra!' I tell him.

OK, it is actually a crop-top, and I only wear it on special occasions because it's kind of uncomfortable and too tight around my arms, but he's not to know that, is he?

'Yeah, right,' he says, giving me a pitying look. 'I don't think you're a teenager at all. I think you're about seven.'

He turns away and hops towards the pool.

I am speechless. It's not fair that a slimy little kid can make me feel so small, so babyish. I take a sneaky look in the changing-room mirror. I don't look like a seven-year-old, do I? I am tall, skinny . . . and pancake-flat.

I remember Beth and Willow telling me I'll understand about them crushing on Ethan when I'm more grown up, and that hurts too.

On impulse, I grab my stripy over-the-knee socks from the locker, slam the door and sneak into the ladies' loo. A bra would be better, obviously, but socks can be quite useful in an emergency. I roll them up and stuff them into the top of my swimsuit, adjusting them until I'm sure they look natural.

I can feel myself standing a little taller already. If Beth and Willow could see me now, they'd never say I was too young to know about crushes and true love. I look grown up – well, apart from the armbands and the two rubber rings. I'll show Frog Boy.

I hold my head high and walk out to the poolside. Frog Boy is in the pool with a bunch of other little kids, splashing around a plump, pink-cheeked instructor. The glinty water, the echoey sound of the pool . . . it makes my heart race and my stomach lurch.

This is not good.

I turn around, ready to make a quick exit, and walk right into a pool attendant with a clipboard and a whistle around his neck. He gives me a funny look, and I tuck the tail end of one stripy sock safely out of sight.

'Daizy Star?' he asks, scanning his clipboard.

76

'We've been waiting for you! I'm Steve and this is Sue . . .' He points towards the pink-cheeked woman in the pool.

'I've changed my mind,' I say. 'This is not a good idea.'

'Come on,' Steve says, laughing. 'We'll have you swimming in no time! Take off the armbands and the rubber rings, though, you won't need them!'

I think of Dad, shelling out for the lessons so we can all sail around the world in a flat-pack boat that may or may not capsize. I'm still having nightmares about it, where I dream it's stormy and dark and I am on watch, wearing my orange waterproof trousers. I see an iceberg looming in the distance, and a wave the size of a house crashes down over me and suddenly I am in the sea. Then a giant octopus grabs my ankles and drags me under, and my bones turn to ice as the water closes above my head . . .

That's when I wake up, of course, shivering and gasping, my heart pounding.

Maybe the nightmares would ease up if I could swim? It could be worth a try. There's Pixie's mermaid party too, which I'm dreading, and school swimming lessons, and the shame of being left out whenever Beth and Willow want to meet up at the pool on a Saturday . . . I need to do this.

I don't want to learn to swim, but I have to try. I take off the armbands, shimmy out of the rubber rings and climb down the steps into the water. I line up with the others, holding on to the handrail. Steve blows his whistle and the lesson begins.

'Kick those legs!' he yells, and an explosion of splashing erupts around me. 'Point those toes and kick . . .'

I adjust the socks, grip the rail and make a few feeble kicks. Sue is moving along the line behind me, helping kids with their technique, but I must be OK because she leaves me alone. I may not be quite as bad as I thought. I am in a new class, where nobody knows me and none of us can swim. Maybe I can do this after all?

'Now,' Steve announces. 'This time, kick your legs as if you are a frog. Feet together, bend your knees, lift your feet up to your bottom . . . then kick out and finish with your legs straight and your knees touching! And repeat!'

There is a frenzy of kicking all around me.

Suddenly, something grabs my ankles, and I'm back in the nightmare. A storm. An iceberg. A giant octopus . . .

I panic, kicking out as hard as I can. There's an endless, ear-splitting scream that even Steve's whistle can't cut through, and after a while I realize that I'm the one who's screaming. I take a deep breath in and open my eyes. Everyone is quiet. Nine Baby Dolphins are staring at me, faintly horrified.

'What do you think you are doing, Daizy?' Steve demands.

'Something grabbed me!' I yelp.

Steve grits his teeth. 'It was Sue, trying to help you with your leg technique. I think you've given her a black eye.'

I turn around slowly. Sue cradles her face in her hands. Blood seeps from one nostril, and from what I can see her eye doesn't look so much black as a mottled crimson/purple mixture.

There was no storm, no iceberg, no giant octopus, just a pink-cheeked teacher, trying to be helpful. And I kicked her in the face.

'Sorry!' I whisper.

Sue climbs out of the pool and stalks across to the lifeguard's office for some first aid. I spend the rest of the lesson clinging to the edge of the pool in shame and despair while the Baby Dolphins take floats and start swimming widths. When Steve blows his whistle to signal the end of the lesson, I am out of there.

'Daizy!' he hisses, as I haul myself up the steps, dripping. 'Your . . . erm . . . scarf, is it?'

That's when I realize. One stripy sock has edged out of the top of my swimsuit to wrap

itself around my
neck like a seaweed
scarf. The other
has slipped right
down and around,
and is trailing like a
tail from the back
of my right
swimsuit leg.

My face
turns beetroot.

'Why has she got a sock around her neck?' one
small girl asks.

'Why has she got a stripy tail?' another
puzzles.

My eyes prickle with tears. I have never been
so embarrassed in my whole, entire life. Kids are
laughing now, and whispering, and even Steve
stifles a smile. I am a stupid, stupid idiot, and
everyone here knows it.

I edge towards the changing rooms, my sock-
tail dropping to the ground as I go.

'Hey!' a slimy, familiar voice yells, and a scrunched-up, sopping-wet sock hits me on the back of the neck. 'Don't forget this!' From the corner of my eye I can see Frog Boy laughing, open-mouthed. Or maybe he's just catching flies?

One thing's for sure, my Baby Dolphin days are over – I am never doing this again. Not as long as I live.

9

I hide in my cubicle for a long time, until my tears have dried and the yells and giggles of the Baby Dolphins have faded. I dress quickly, shivering. My stripy socks are clammy and stink of chlorine, but I pull them on anyway. And, yes, this time I am wearing them on my feet.

My shoes make a squelching noise as I walk, but I hold my head high. I make it through the changing rooms and across the lobby. I'm through the double doors and halfway down the steps before I hear it . . . an ear-splitting wolf whistle.

Nothing to do with me, obviously. I hope.

'Daizy! Daizy, wait up!
I've come to walk you
home!'

I turn around and
there is Becca, picking
her way down the steps
in her biker boots,
school bag swinging.
Her lips are blood red
and her hair glints
purple in the afternoon
sun, and that is not
the colour it was this
morning, I swear.

'Right.' I take a
deep breath in. 'What
happened to
your hair? And
did you . . .
were you . . .
watching
the lesson?'

Becca laughs. 'It's just a spray-in colour. And no, we weren't watching – I'm sure you were very good, but we got here a bit late . . . thought we'd missed you!'

We?

For the first time, I notice a boy lurking on the steps behind her. He is tall and gruff and faintly menacing, in a long black coat and fingerless gloves. His black hair is streaked with green and hangs down over his face so that it almost hides the metal stud that sticks out beneath his bottom lip. Almost, but not quite.

It might just be the shock of the worst-ever swimming lesson catching up with me, but he makes me feel slightly queasy.

'This is Spike,' Becca says.

'Er . . . hello, Spike,' I squeak out.

'All right,' he growls.

My sister is hanging

out with a scary goth gorilla with mouldering hair and a pierced lip. Why am I not surprised?

'So,' Becca asks, steering me up towards the high street, with Spike trailing along behind. 'Good lesson?'

'Not really. I made a complete fool of myself.'

Becca raises an eyebrow. 'Want to talk about it?'

'No,' I say firmly. 'Not now. Not later. Not in a million years. And I am never, ever, EVER going back.'

'Oh, come on,' Becca says. 'We all make mistakes. It's never as bad as you think.'

'It's worse,' I tell her. 'I promise.'

'Well, even if it was, you can still get over it,' she insists. 'For my sake.'

I blink. 'What d'you mean?'

Becca rolls her eyes. 'Dad is being so strict and stressy,' she tells me. 'It's probably part of the mid-life-crisis thing. He says I can't go out on school nights, which is just totally unfair.'

'You never used to go out,' I remind her. 'It didn't bother you.'

86

'Well, it does now,' Becca sniffs. 'I have to see Spike – I just HAVE to. We might not have long together, what with this crazy sailing-round-the-world idea. As soon as Dad finishes that stupid boat, my life is over . . . so right now, I can't afford to waste a minute.'

'I suppose.'

Becca lowers her voice. 'Besides . . . Dad's not exactly going to approve of Spike, is he?'

I take a quick look over my shoulder. Beneath the green, floppy fringe I'm sure I can see smudges of eyeliner. Yikes.

'Probably not,' I say. 'Definitely, absolutely, totally not. In fact, no way.'

'It's a problem,' Becca agrees. 'But you can help, Daizy! If you keep going swimming, I can hang out with Spike and walk you home at the same time, twice a week! Dad won't suspect a thing!'

'But . . .'

'For me, Daizy?' Becca begs. 'Just keep going to this Little Whales class . . .'

'Baby Dolphins,' I huff.

'Whatever. And don't tell Dad about Spike, OK? Please?' Beneath the crimped purple fringe, my big sister's eyes brim with tears. She looks lost, lonely, a tragic heroine in biker boots and black nail varnish, and my heart melts.

'Well . . .'

Becca grins. 'Thanks, Daizy, I knew you wouldn't let me down!'

'I don't want to lie about it,' I say anxiously.

'So don't lie.' Becca gives me a little hug. 'Just keep going to the lessons, and don't mention Spike. What do you think of him, anyway?'

I give the lanky green-fringed goth a long, hard look. 'Are you really called Spike?' I ask him.

'Sure he is,' Becca says.

'Well,' Spike corrects her. 'My real name is Sebastian Pyke, but I think Spike suits me better.'

I think he may be right about that.

'Where did you meet?'

'School orchestra,' Spike says. 'I play the

cello.' His voice is gruff, but very quiet and polite, and although he looks fierce, his eyes are quite twinkly. Besides, he plays the cello. He may not be quite as scary as he looks.

Becca and Spike linger at the corner of Silver Street, kissing goodbye, which is kind of cringey and probably unhygienic too. Think of all those germs. If this is what growing up involves, I'm not interested, seriously.

'Daizy!' Dad beams as I skulk into the house. 'How was Baby Dolphins?'

'Fine,' I say. Becca comes in, nodding encouragement. 'Great, in fact,' I rush on. 'I don't know what all the fuss was about.'

I am shocked at how easily the lies slip off my tongue. Baby Dolphins was not fine, not fine at all. I'll keep on going to the pool . . . for Becca's sake. I just won't go to the lessons. I'll hide out in the leisure centre cafe and learn my spellings and think about my star quality, but nothing will ever get me back into that pool.

I don't need to swim, after all, to sail around

89

the world. I just need to hang on tight and make sure I don't fall in.

Sorted.

Later that week, a lorry draws up outside our house and two men stride up the path and ring the bell. Becca answers the door and gives the delivery men a forbidding glare.

'Haddock for number fifty-three Silver Street?' the men ask. Becca huffs and tells them we didn't order a takeaway, but Dad just elbows his way through and signs the delivery sheet and goes out to help them unload.

The rest of us watch from the window as dozens of huge boxes and endless vast, random plywood shapes are taken from the lorry and carried across the front lawn. A gigantic tree trunk follows . . . the mast, I suppose.

When the lorry trundles away, we go outside and gawp. The carport is stuffed to bursting with boxes and packages, and Dad unfolds a big chart showing how the *Haddock* is put together.

'You can all help,' he tells us, as if this is a special treat.

'I'll be busy,' Becca says. 'I can't fall behind with my homework, can I? Not if you're dragging me out of school to sail around the world in this heap of junk. You don't want to wreck my future career, as well as my social life, do you?'

'Becca!' Dad says warningly.

'Well, I'm busy,' she rushes on. 'On Mondays and Thursdays I have to walk Daizy home from Baby Dolphins. On Tuesday it's orchestra, on Wednesday it's advanced maths and on Friday it's choir practice.'

Maybe Becca does still go to orchestra, but I think that advanced maths has probably been replaced by Kissing for Beginners. As for choir practice, I think it's more Spike and Becca sharing an iPod and singing along.

'I'm sure you can fit us in somewhere,' Dad says. 'How about Saturday?'

'On Saturday I'm going out,' Becca snaps.

I sit down on a cardboard box, head in hands. My family is unravelling, and we haven't even started on the boat-building yet. How are we going to cope when we're hundreds of miles out to sea, just the five of us, surviving on instant soup and dried biscuits? It doesn't bear thinking about.

One large *Haddock*, coming up.

I can hardly wait.

10

Mr Smart takes forever to decide about the designs for the adventure playground, but finally he does – and he picks my shipwreck idea. When Miss Moon tells me, I am so shocked and excited that my mouth just opens and closes like a fish. This is not a good look, even if it is in keeping with the watery theme.

'Well done, Daizy,' Miss Moon says. 'The infant classes loved your ideas. They are going to have a wonderful time playing pirates and walking the plank and finding the buried treasure.'

'I had a lot of help,' I remind her. 'It was a team effort.'

'Maybe,' she says. 'But the idea was yours. Next, Mr Smart will talk to the council about your design. They will look at safety issues and draw up plans . . . and we can start raising funds to help it become a reality! Does anyone have any fundraising ideas?'

'Why not give everything a watery theme?' Willow suggests. 'To fit with Daizy's design? We could have an Under-the-Sea Disco, with collaged starfish and fake seaweed draped around the walls . . .' She flutters her lashes at Ethan, who looks a little scared.

'Good idea,' Miss Moon says. 'A watery-themed disco – for the parents, perhaps?'

Willow looks deflated, Ethan relieved.

'How about a raffle?' Kelly Munroe offers. 'The prize could be a treasure chest, full of chocolate coins and brightly coloured sweets and those necklaces you can get that are made of candy . . .'

'Terrific,' Miss Moon

says. 'Any other ideas?'

Yasmin puts her hand up. 'A sponsored walk?'

'That's not very watery,' Freya says.

There's a silence, and Yasmin's shoulders slump.

'Well, make it a sponsored swim . . .' The words are out of my mouth before I can stop them, and now it's too late. The idea is out there, and it's the worst I've ever had in my whole entire life.

'Brilliant,' Beth says.

'It'd be fun.'

'Let's do it!'

'You're full of good ideas, Daizy Star,' Miss Moon says. 'Fantastic! Every child in the juniors can collect sponsor money! We'll hire the pool for the day and get the papers along for publicity – we might get some extra donations that way. What do you think?'

Willow puts her hand up. 'We can add all the lengths together and work out how far we've swum,' she suggests. 'Like . . . Brighton, or Paris, or . . . Timbuktu?'

'We could call it the Big Swim. Or Swim Around the World!' Freya declares.

I put my head in my hands. Swimming around the world? I didn't think anything could be worse than sailing around the world, but I was wrong.

'OK, Daizy?' Murphy Malone whispers.

'Never better,' I lie.

Murphy puts his hand in the air. 'What about the kids who can't swim so well?' he asks. 'Won't they feel a bit left out?'

'We'll make sure everyone is an important part of this,' Miss Moon promises. 'Non-swimmers can still take part, with armbands or floats or whatever – it's all about doing your own personal best.'

Miss Moon starts planning possible dates for the disco, the raffle and the Big Swim. She divides the class into groups, making posters and decorations, designing tickets and sponsorship forms and drafting a letter to the newspaper. Everybody gets stuck in, full of ideas and enthusiasm.

Everyone except me.

I sit quietly, making a collage starfish out of card and tissue paper. It's going quite well, until Beth points out that starfish only have five pointy bits and mine has seventeen, and I get huffy and scrunch it up and chuck it in the bin.

I'm still feeling gloomy later, walking home with Murphy and Pixie. Pixie is skipping on ahead, trying not to stand on the cracks in the paving stones.

'You must be pleased about your shipwreck design,' Murphy says, trying to cheer me up. 'It's going to be awesome!'

'I suppose.'

'The fundraising should be fun,' Murphy says. 'I was surprised you suggested a sponsored swim, though.'

I was a bit surprised myself, but I can't tell Murphy that. I will just have to think of a way out of the mess – a sudden fever or an all-over rash that means I have to stay in bed all day, perhaps. My mind starts plotting. A thermometer dipped in a hot cup of tea? A face full of red spots dabbed on with poster paint?

'Dad signed me up for that class, remember?' I remind Murphy brightly. 'Success guaranteed. I'll probably be swimming like a fish by then.'

Murphy grins. 'That's great. It takes courage to conquer a fear like that. You're some girl, Daizy Star.'

Some idiot, more like. We're in Silver Street, and Pixie is swinging on the garden gate, waiting for us to catch up.

'I didn't stand on a single crack in the pavement,' she tells us. 'Not one!'

'That's good,' I say. 'What happens if you do?'

'Something really, really terrible,' she says firmly.

That's great. I must have stepped on about a million.

11

As if things could get any worse, the Big Swim is scheduled to take place the day of Pixie's birthday. Two terrifying events in one day . . . perfect, huh?

Pixie has been busy designing mermaid-themed invites and asking all her friends along. She is so excited about the party, she may actually explode before it actually rolls around.

Pixie Star invites you . . . . to a party . . . . on . . . . at . . . . R.S.V.P.

Any plans I had of pulling a sickie and staying in bed all day are clearly not happening now – I

can't let Pixie down, can I? I'll just have to think
of something else.

Soon.

A whole bunch of nightmares about
swimming to Timbuktu or playing pass the parcel
underwater start to liven up my nights, in
between the usual octopus/iceberg/shark-attack
dreams. It's all very worrying.

Still, nothing can take away the buzz of
knowing my shipwreck idea is going to be the
theme for the new adventure playground. Being
picked for Star of the Week would be cooler still
. . . I must be in with a good chance now, surely?
Miss Moon did say I was full of good ideas, and
suggesting a sponsored swim must count for
something too, even if it is the worst idea in the
history of the universe.

I could be Star of the Week, I really could.

Yeah, right.

On Friday morning, Ali Hamood rescues a
kitten from the canal on the way into school.
A reporter from the *Evening News* comes to school

to take his photo, and of course Miss Moon makes Ali Star of the Week.

Ali Hamood

Typical.

Dad has dismantled Pixie's swing to make space in the back garden. Now when you look out there you can see the framework of the *Haddock* taking shape, like the skeleton of a whale.

Dad works from dawn till dusk, sawing, sanding and clamping bits of wood together. He gets Bert from next door to help him, and the two of them spend hours poring over plans and charts, sipping tea and shaking their heads. Then they measure the boat and fiddle about with the spirit level and shake their heads again.

Today, Dad and Bert have begun to fit the hull around the framework. It's a little bit lumpy and uneven in places, like a larger version of the model boats we made in Year Four, out of string and balsawood and Blu-tack. We took them down to the canal for a test run, and every single one of them sank.

I'm sure things will be different for the *Haddock*.

Pixie and I have been roped in to help hold a panel in place while Dad and Bert nail it down. The trouble is, the panel doesn't seem to fit, so we do a lot of standing around holding the thing while Dad and Bert huff and grumble and consult the plans again.

'We might need to steam it,' Dad says.

'Perhaps if we trimmed this pointy bit down and tacked an extra bit on the far end?' Bert muses.

Pixie and I exchange looks. This could take some time.

Becca saunters out into the garden with mugs of tea for Dad and Bert. The purple dye has long since washed out, but still, she looks as if she applied her make-up in the dark, and combed her hair in a gale-force wind, using a forked twig.

'Is it meant to look like that?' she asks, eyeing the *Haddock*.

Dad frowns. 'Like what?'

'Like you've botched it together from old packing crates and broken floorboards,' Becca says. 'Is that gap meant to be there?'

'We haven't finished that bit. Obviously.'

'You can't have a gap in the hull when you're building a boat,' Becca points out. 'Water will come in.'

'I know that!' Dad snaps.

'This panel won't fit, either,' Pixie pipes up.

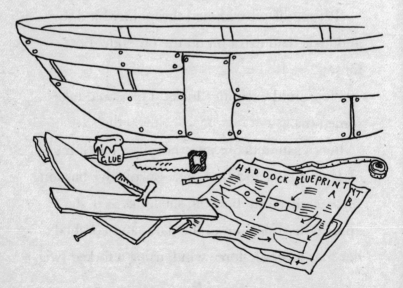

'Pixie, shhh!' I hiss. I don't want Dad getting any more wound up. He could explode at any moment, seriously.

'We're having trouble with the plans,' Bert-from-next-door admits. 'Complicated, they are.'

'Or maybe Dad's just not very good at woodwork,' Becca says.

'Young lady, haven't you got homework to do?'

'Nope.'

'Revision then?' Dad grumbles. 'Your hair looks like you've just crawled out of a bramble bush. Tie it back, can't you?'

'I like it like this,' Becca grins.

Dad puts down his hammer and gives Becca a stern look. It's his geography-teacher look – an arctic glare that can reduce spotty Year Nine thugs to mush at fifty paces. Unless they are planning to set the world on fire, of course.

Dad must be losing his touch, lately, because it doesn't work on Becca, either.

'Tie your hair back,' he says grimly. 'I can't even see your face these days. Although you're wearing so much make-up I doubt I'd recognize you anyway! What must your teachers think?'

'Who cares?' Becca shrugs.

'You used to care!' Dad says.

'I used to have a life too,' Becca snaps. 'But you put paid to all that. My friends pity me, do you know that? Don't expect me to care about teachers, Dad. Why should I?'

We are not the kind of family who have loud, in-your-face arguments in the back garden, in front of the neighbours. Until now. Pixie stares, fascinated, while I chew my lip in distress.

'Tie your hair back,' Dad repeats, and Becca just sighs and pulls the curtain of hair back from her face.

I blink. My sister Becca has a small silver stud piercing her right nostril.

Dad stares, horrified, and Bert-from-next-door coughs and says his lunch will be ready about now, making a hasty exit. Pixie's eyes have gone round and huge, and she digs me in the ribs with a sharp elbow.

'Get. To. Your. Room,' Dad says slowly and painfully. 'NOW!'

Becca rolls her eyes and turns away. 'By the way,' she says, over her shoulder. 'That panel is upside down.'

Dad just glares, and turns to the panel. 'Ridiculous,' he mutters.

He stomps into the house.

Pixie and I lift the panel and turn it the other way up, holding it into place against the frame.

It's a perfect fit.

My sister Becca is grounded for life, or at least until her pierced nose has healed up. That might take a long time, because whenever Dad is not around she puts the stud back in. She does it now, walking down Silver Street with me and Pixie on Monday morning.

'Don't the teachers mind?' Pixie wants to know.

Becca laughs. 'Of course not. Dad is so old-fashioned! He's ruining my life. How am I supposed to see Spike now?'

'Spike?' Pixie echoes.

'Her boyfriend,' I explain. 'He has green hair, eyeliner and a pierced lip.'

'Cool,' Pixie breathes. 'Bring him round to the house! We can watch my *Little Mermaid* DVD.'

'That sounds lovely,' Becca says. 'Thanks, Pixie. But there's no way Dad is meeting him! If he flipped out over one tiny nose stud, I dread to think what he'd make of Spike . . .'

Becca has a point. If Dad finds out about Spike it'd just about finish him off. He'd probably sail us directly to a desert island and maroon us all there forever, far away from boys with piercings and friends with names like Skidd, Razz and Ziggy.

'Can Spike come to my birthday party?' Pixie

begs. 'Please? Dad would have to be nice to him then.'

'Well, maybe,' Becca considers. 'After all, Dad wouldn't need to know that he was my boyfriend. We'll see. Me and Spike can still pick you up from Baby Dolphins later, can't we, Daizy? Dad can't stop me from doing that. You are still going?'

'Of course,' I say through gritted teeth. 'I wouldn't miss it for the world . . .'

F reya Jenks is made Star of the
Week for bringing in chocolate
krispie cakes for everyone in
class. I wish I'd thought of
that. How are you
supposed to guess what
might make you Star
of the Week?
It's very puzzling.

I have enough on my mind as it is.

Life is getting seriously complicated. Beth and
Willow are planning a sleepover, and they want
to hold it at my place.

'The last one was at mine,' Willow says. 'And

the one before that was at Beth's, so it's your turn. OK?'

'Well . . .'

Beth frowns. 'Daizy?' she says. 'Is it OK? Or not?'

'Um . . . not,' I squeak out.

There's an uncomfortable silence.

'We never see you out of school, these days,' Willow says. 'It's ages since you asked us for tea or anything.'

'I've been busy!'

'Busy? Doing what?'

Building a boat, I think gloomily, but I can't say that, of course.

A guilty blush creeps up my cheeks. 'Mum's been working late shifts,' I bluff. 'And Dad's doing some . . . some woodwork. The house is a bit of a mess.'

There are wood shavings on the carpet and a lopsided *Haddock* in the back garden, but I can't go into detail. Beth and Willow exchange glances, and I know right away that Ethan Miller is not their only topic of conversation these days.

They have been talking about this. About me.
A lump forms in my throat, sharp and scratchy,
like a sliver of glass.

At least we've got each other,' Willow tells
Beth, and I can barely believe my ears. Am I
losing my best friends now, as well as everything
else?

'You've got me too!' I argue.

Beth sniffs. 'Well . . . if you're sure you're not
too busy.'

'I'm not!' I insist. 'Things are a bit awkward at
home just now, that's all.'

Willow softens. 'Do you want to talk about it?'
she asks.

'No!' I bark. 'I mean, yes, but not just yet. It's
. . . complicated.'

My life is one big knot of secrets and lies . . .
and if you pull too hard, the whole thing might
just unravel.

On Thursday I sit in the sports-centre cafe for

ages, with Murphy's skull-print scarf draped around my head like a hijab. I am in disguise, obviously. The Baby Dolphins flounder around in the pool below while I study my spellings and try to come up with a foolproof plan to get me out of the sponsored swim.

On Monday I huddle in the corner in a hoody and a baseball cap, trying to make a flapjack and lemonade last for an hour and stitching away at the life-size mermaid's tail I am making for Pixie's birthday. It's quite cool, in a fishy, scaly

kind of a way. It's made from an old dress of Mum's, all sea-green silk and silvery stitching. I am sewing on scales made from silver foil for a bit of extra sparkle.

The cafe lady comes over to my table to wipe away the flapjack crumbs and rattle my lemonade can to see if it's empty. 'You can't have that . . . that tail in here,' she sniffs. 'It's against the rules.'

'There's a rule about no tails in the cafe?' I raise one eyebrow. 'Seriously?'

She glares. 'You're getting silver foil all over my nice clean floor.'

Nobody susses I haven't really been swimming, though. I remember to rinse my swimsuit under the tap in the ladies' loo in case Mum spots that it's still dry, and I splash my hair so that it's all ringlety and damp. It fools Becca and Spike, and it fools Mum, Dad and Pixie too.

'Good lesson?' they ask, and I tell them I've made a real impression on the instructors. It's true . . . just not the way my family imagine.

On the Thursday of what should have been my last Baby Dolphin lesson, I have a stroke of luck. I am skulking down the stairs past the changing rooms wearing Mum's floppy gardening hat and a lime-green scarf from the school lost-property box, happy that Monday and Thursday afternoons will no longer be spent holed up in the sports-centre cafe. Then I spot a small blue badge on the floor at my feet.

I bend and pick it up.

It's one of those woven badges you're meant to stitch on to your swimsuit, to prove that you can swim – and embroidered on to the blue background is a leaping dolphin.

Perfect.

'How did you get on?' Becca asks when she and Spike come to collect me. 'Today was your last lesson – did you pass?'

I show her the badge, and I only feel a tiny bit guilty when she tells Spike that I am the cleverest

kid in the world. If I was that clever, I'd have
figured out a way to wriggle out of the sponsored
swim while still being around for Pixie's party.
I'm working on it, though.

Back home, Mum has made a celebration tea,
with cheesy pasta and chocolate cake, and orange
juice and lemonade in tall glasses, with umbrellas
in the top. I can barely choke down any of it, I
feel so guilty.

'We're proud of you,' Mum says. 'Well done!'

'It's a real achievement,' Dad tells me.
'Congratulations!'

'Daizy,' Pixie says, 'you are a star!'

I wish.

Right now, my only star quality seems to be lying . . .

13

Everything is ready for Pixie's birthday. Becca has made the mermaid cake, shaping pieces of sponge and sticking them together with buttercream before hiding the joins beneath layers of coloured icing. It looks amazing. We are keeping it in a tin in Bert-from-next-door's kitchen, so as not to spoil the surprise. Mum is planning to make about a million sandwiches, plus a vast green jelly with fish-shaped sweets set inside it.

Pixie's present is almost ready. I have to work on it when Pixie is not around, or sneak out to the cabin of the *Haddock* and stitch it there, by torchlight. It is stitched and tapered like a real

mermaid's tail, so Pixie can wriggle into it and pose on the side of the pool and imagine how it feels to be a mermaid for a day. I have stuffed the tail with the insides of two old pillows, and put elastic at the top so it fits around your waist.

Pixie has ten friends coming, some from school and some from Little Seals, all with an adult in tow to make sure they stay safe. Spike is coming too – if anyone asks, Becca is planning to pass him off as somebody's big brother.

'Can we ask Murphy?' Pixie wants to know.

I'd love to invite Beth and Willow and Murphy, but there's no way I can risk it at the moment – what if someone mentioned the *Haddock*, or sailing around the world?

'I don't think Murphy will be able to make it,' I bluff, feeling really mean and guilty. 'He's busy that afternoon. Definitely.'

Pixie looks disappointed, but still, she is counting down the days. I'm counting too. I finally have a plan to escape the sponsored swim . . .

119

I never did like rollerblades. They may be all clumpy and heavy, but you can't trust them – they might slither off in a hundred different directions, without any warning at all.

Just what I need.

I dig Becca's old blades out from the back of the cupboard and strap them on.

'Are you mad?' Becca asks. 'You're rubbish on those. You have no sense of balance.'

'I'm going to learn,' I say grimly. 'I am going to conquer all my fears. First swimming, now rollerblades . . .'

'You'll have a pet worm next,' Becca says.

'Ewww. I don't think so.'

I slither up and down the hallway a few times experimentally. It's not as bad as I remember.

'Look,' Becca says. 'Are you sure about this? I can't hang around. I'm meeting Spike by the sweetshop.'

'I'll be fine!'

I clomp down the garden path after Becca and Pixie, my schoolbag swinging. 'Wait for me!' I yell. 'Hold on . . . urghhh!'

I collide with next-door's rose bush, and Murphy Malone legs it across the road to rescue me. 'Rollerblades, for school?' he asks, hauling me upright again. 'Is that a good idea?'

'I am looking for my star quality,' I inform him. 'It could be rollerblades, right?'

'Wrong,' Murphy says as I lurch off the pavement and into the gutter. 'Look, Daizy, hang on to me, or we'll never get to school.'

'It's a shame you're busy on my birthday, Murphy,' Pixie pipes up. 'I really wanted you to come to my mermaid party.'

'What day is your birthday?' Murphy asks.

'Tomorrow,' Pixie tells him. 'The party is right after school.'

Murphy grins. 'That sounds great,' he says. 'I'm not busy at all. I'll be there, Pixie. You can count on it.'

'But Daizy said –'

'Help!!!!' I yell, wobbling about a bit
and sliding into the gutter to distract Pixie. By
the time they've hauled me out and brushed me
down, Pixie has forgotten my fib about Murphy
being busy. I am off the hook – for now.

Except that Murphy is going to come
to the party. What if he finds out that I've been
hiding the biggest thing that's ever happened
to me from him? I don't even want to think
about it.

It takes forever to get to Stella Street Primary,
with Murphy propping me up on one side and
Pixie on the other. Beth and Willow run over to
see what I'm doing, and even Ethan Miller looks
up from his footy game.

'What's this all about?' Beth hisses. 'People are
looking, Daizy!'

'I'm just trying to improve my technique . . .'

'You don't have a technique,' Murphy says
kindly. 'Sorry, Daizy – blading is not your star
quality.'

'C'mon, Daizy,' Willow says. 'This is slightly embarrassing . . .'

Embarrassing? Willow doesn't know the meaning of the word. This is nothing.

'I can do it,' I protest, shaking them all off. 'I . . . yeeeow!!!!'

I hurtle across the playground at an alarming speed, slicing through a skipping game and scattering a whole bunch of Year Threes who are playing hopscotch. Then my legs seem to slide in different directions, and I land on my bum in the middle of the footy game, right at Ethan Miller's feet.

'Daizy Star,' he says, laughing. 'I know I am irresistible to girls, but you don't have to throw yourself at me!'

'Shut up, Ethan,' I snap.

Pixie, Murphy, Beth and Willow crowd around to see if I'm OK. I wrench off the rollerblades and pull a face.

'My ankle!' I groan. 'I think I've twisted it!'
Rollerblading is not my star quality, I know that,

but how about acting? I think I'm doing OK.

I stagger to my feet, hobbling slightly.

Suddenly, Ethan Miller elbows my friends aside, grabs me around the waist, flings me over his shoulder and marches off towards the school building.

'Ethan!' I yell. 'You idiot! Put me down! NOW!!!!'

'You need help,' Ethan grunts. 'That ankle could be nasty.'

Forget the ankle – *I* could be nasty, if Ethan Miller doesn't put me down. 'Stop it!' I scream, wriggling and kicking and flailing my arms. 'Beth! Willow! Do something!'

My friends exchange dark glances.

'Honestly!' Willow says. 'Some people would do anything to get attention!'

They scowl at me and walk away.

Ethan barges right through the double doors and comes to a halt abruptly just outside the staffroom, dumping me to the ground like a sack of potatoes. 'We need a doctor,' he yells, hammering on the door. 'Daizy's hurt her ankle!'

'I've hurt everything else as well, thanks to you,' I scowl. 'You've just about shaken me to death!'

Miss Moon appears in the doorway, and Ethan prods me gently with one sparkly-white trainer before swaggering back to the playground.

'So, Daizy, what seems to be the problem?' Miss Moon asks kindly, and I wonder where to begin, because there are so many problems it doesn't bear thinking about. Then I realize that she's talking about my ankle. I sit down on a bench under the coathooks while Miss Moon takes a look at it. It isn't red or swollen, and Miss

Moon says she's sure it isn't broken. I won't need an X-ray.

'You may have sprained it,' she tells me. 'Keep your weight off it for a couple of days and see your doctor if it doesn't ease up. And stay away from those rollerblades!'

'What about the Big Swim tomorrow?' I ask, trying to sound anxious. 'What if . . .'

'We'll see,' Miss Moon says. 'But it's not looking good, I'm afraid.'

I have to agree – it's not looking good at all. I may have got myself out of the sponsored swim, but my two best friends have gone all huffy on me again, and *that* hurts. Ethan Miller has a lot to answer for.

I head off down the corridor sadly, remembering to limp.

On Pixie's birthday, I hobble downstairs, groaning. My ankle is cocooned in bandage from the first-aid box in the bathroom. It looks like I have a watermelon under my stripy socks.

'Daizy!' Dad exclaims. 'Your poor ankle!'

'It's worse,' I tell him. 'All swollen and sore.' My fingers are crossed behind my back, so it doesn't really count as a lie.

Last night, Mum checked me over and said

that sprains could be nasty, even if there was no swelling or bruising. She made me sit for hours with my leg up on the sofa, with a packet of frozen peas wrapped in a tea towel strapped to my foot.

I could have got frostbite, seriously.

The trouble with having a nurse for a mum is that you can't get away with things easily, not when those things are body-related. A nurse might see through the act and decide that there's nothing wrong with you, or, worse, that you need to be rushed to casualty right away.

I couldn't take any risks. I decided to go mad with the bandaging and hope that Mum would be too busy doing birthday stuff with Pixie to unravel it and prod at my ankle all over again.

It seems to be working.

Mum is busy making breakfast while my little sister skips around her like a whirlwind, opening presents and shrieking with glee. 'A mermaid doll! I always wanted one of those! A Slinky! Wow, a charm bracelet . . . with a mermaid charm, and a boat, and a fish, and a seahorse! Look, Daizy!'

'It's beautiful,' I say. 'Happy birthday, Pixie!'

'I'm seven!' Pixie trills.

'I know. Just wait till your party, later . . . you can have my pressie then! It's a surprise!'

Becca appears, all smudgy eyeliner and crimped hair, and hands a large, silver-wrapped package to Pixie. It turns out to be orange flippers, which sets Pixie off squealing all over again.

Dad brings in the post, mostly cards and parcels from Gran and Grandad for Pixie. 'Have you seen Daizy's ankle, Liv?' he asks.

'Ouch,' Mum says, glancing down at my foot. 'I was sure that the cold compress last night would do the trick. Shall I take a look?'

'Don't worry,' I tell her. 'I put on a bandage. I'll still be OK for the Big Swim, won't I?'

Mum shakes her head slowly. 'I don't think so, love,' she says. 'No swimming for you.'

I pull a face, but inside I am jumping for joy.

'After all your hard work at the Baby Dolphins too!' Dad says. 'I know how much you wanted to show us what you'd learnt!'

'I'm sorry, Daizy,' Mum says.

Maybe she is, but I'm not.

Result!!!

The Big Swim is going well.

The younger classes go first, class by class, their teachers totting up the total of lengths and widths. Miss Moon tells us how far a width is in actual metres, and how far a length is, in actual metres, and asks us to work out how far our school has swum altogether.

My head aches with the effort, just like when we have maths questions about dividing up cakes and sharing hundreds of lemons between a certain number of people. I always want to suggest that they should just take one slice each, and whizz up the lemons with some sugar to make lemonade. But that's not the right thing to put, I know, because the answer is always a fraction or a decimal or some other long and complicated number.

Murphy works out that the total distance swum so far is 3.78 kilometres, which sounds pretty unimpressive, even to me. They should have shipped Pixie in from the infant class, because I bet she could swim a kilometre all by herself.

In the afternoon, it's our turn. We are the oldest class, with the strongest swimmers, and we have all afternoon to notch up a few more kilometres. We file out to the poolside, everyone in swimsuits and shorts . . . except for me. I've been asked to look after the refreshment table, which means topping up the orange squash and arranging the biscuits in pretty patterns. It beats floundering around in the pool, anyhow.

There's just one problem – Beth and Willow. Ever since the rollerblade fiasco, they've been acting moody, mean and not at all sympathetic. I looked at Becca's magazines again, and they said that hormones can cause irrational mood swings at puberty.

Poor Beth. Poor Willow. I *think*.

'Shame you're missing out,' Beth says, not sounding sorry at all. 'Especially now you can finally swim.'

'Your ankle looks sore,' Willow chimes in. 'And weird.'

'Gee, thanks,' I quip.

'We did warn you,' she says sniffily. 'That whole rollerblade thing was mad. You were showing off, Daizy, trying to impress Ethan.

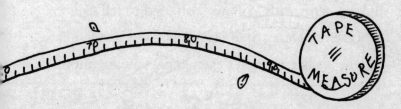

And he's so nice he was taken in by it!'

I blink. 'Er, no!' I protest. 'That's not how it was!'

'So how was it?' Beth asks, but of course, I can't answer that. A fake rollerblading accident? An imaginary sprained ankle? It all sounds kind of crazy.

Beth raises an eyebrow. 'Whatever,' she says, linking arms with Willow. 'You used to tell us everything, Daizy Star . . . but you've changed. Lately, it's like we don't even know you any more!'

My eyes sting with tears. I watch Beth and Willow walk away and I want to call after them, tell them about the ankle and the swimming and the *Haddock* in the garden, but I don't know where to start. I don't know if they'd listen, or even care.

The two of them slide into the water, giggling and fluttering their lashes at Ethan Miller. Miss Moon blows a whistle and the swimmers are off, thrashing their way up and down the pool while she adds up the lengths in her notebook.

I slump at the refreshment table, filling paper cups and wondering how my life got so muddled. Right about when I started keeping secrets and telling lies, I guess, but I'm in too deep to back out now. Aren't I?

Ethan Miller hauls himself out of the water and swaggers over for a drink, grinning. He's been swimming for ages, but his spiky hair is still vertical, as if held in place by superglue.

'Twenty lengths,' he tells me, dripping steadily on to the biscuits. 'Not bad, eh?'

'Suppose.'

'How's the ankle?' he asks.

'Fine,' I sigh. That much, at least, is true.

'Sorry about yesterday,' Ethan says. 'I over-did the heroics a bit, but I was only trying to help.'

'I know,' I tell him. 'Thanks. I guess.'

Maybe Ethan Miller is not as bad as I thought? Then again, maybe he's worse.

'Pity you're not swimming,' he smirks. 'I was looking forward to seeing you in your bikini!'

I shudder. 'I don't own a bikini,' I tell him. 'And if I did, you'd be the last person on earth I'd want to see me in it. Ewww.'

'Why?' Ethan wants to know. 'I don't mind you seeing me in my swim shorts!' He strikes a pose, flexing his arms to show off imaginary muscles.

It's enough to put you off your Jammie Dodgers, seriously.

I catch sight of Beth and Willow, huddled at

the poolside, stony-faced.
I want to tell them I don't
care about Ethan
Miller, that he's a
vain, vacant,
footy-mad
lout with a
fixation for
hair gel and
worms, but
they wouldn't listen.

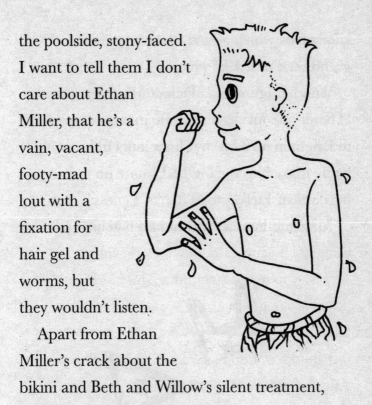

Apart from Ethan
Miller's crack about the
bikini and Beth and Willow's silent treatment,
the afternoon is a great success.

'It's a shame the *Evening News* didn't turn up,'
Miss Moon sighs. 'A piece in the paper could
have pulled in a bit more money. Still, we can't
complain. Well done, Year Six! You've all been
wonderful!'

Murphy makes some quick calculations and
announces that Year Six have swum 3.32

kilometres, which added to the rest gives a grand total of 7.1 kilometres.

'Another great idea, Daizy,' Miss Moon says. 'Thank you. We haven't quite managed to swim to Brighton or Paris or Timbuktu, but we could easily make it to the big B&Q store on the outskirts of Basingstoke . . .'

Amazing. And all without even getting my feet wet . . .

15

Pixie's mermaid birthday party is in full swing. I've changed out of my uniform into a green top and ruffled skirt, but I feel a bit overdressed when everyone else is in swimsuits. My stripy socks and bandaged ankle don't help matters, but still, I'm in a party mood.

I didn't even have to worry about Beth and Willow finding out about the party – neither of them even bothered to say goodbye as the kids from Stella Street Primary left.

On the poolside, the squash-and-biscuits table from earlier has been covered with a bright cloth and laden with plates of pizza and sausages on sticks.

The green jelly shivers under the
bright lights and Becca's mermaid
cake sits in pride of place.

Music pumps out at full blast –
even the lifeguard has perked up. Small
children are laughing, yelling and
splashing all over the shallow end of the
pool, which has been cordoned off and filled
with floats and rafts in half a dozen rainbow
shades.

Murphy is clowning around in Pixie's new
orange flippers and even Spike is lurking in the
background, wearing black skull-print shorts
that come down past his knees, a black mesh
vest and black fingerless gloves.

'Who is that boy?' Mum asks, frowning.

'Do we know him?' Dad wonders.

'He's Charlotte's big
brother,' Becca chips in,
giving me a meaningful
look. I think this might be
true, except that as far as I

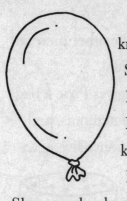

know, Charlotte is a spotty Year
Seven kid, and she is not at
Pixie's mermaid party. Luckily,
Mum and Dad don't seem to
know this.

Pixie is in mermaid heaven.
She squeals when she sees the cake and is almost
speechless when I unveil the mermaid's tail. She
spends ages hopping about the side of the pool in
it and posing with the tail
curled around her, like a
mermaid on a rock.
She says it's her best
present ever, and
gives me a big hug,
leaving soggy handprints
on my new party top.

Some of the other presents are . . . unusual.

Murphy gives Pixie a bag of custard doughnuts, and Spike hands over a live newt in a jam jar,

which makes Mum scream. Pixie loves it and says she's going to call it Nigel.

'Are you sure he's not some dodgy friend of Becca's?' Dad grumbles from the poolside. 'I don't like the look of him. Kids today are so . . . worrying. The sooner we leave all this behind, the better!'

Murphy sits down next to me on a white plastic chair, dripping wet and wearing orange flippers.

'What did your dad mean?' he asks me. 'The sooner we leave all this behind, the better?'

Ah.

'You know Dad,' I bluff. 'Always talking junk.'

Murphy gives me a hard look. 'You're hiding something, Daizy Star. You've been acting strangely for weeks. Is everything OK?'

'Everything's fine,' I insist.

'Beth and Willow have noticed too,' Murphy says. 'We're all really worried.'

'Beth and Willow aren't even talking to me,' I wail. 'They're all huffy because I haven't asked them for a sleepover lately, and because I crashed into Ethan yesterday. They think I like him. And they think I'm being secretive and now they don't want to be friends any more . . .' My eyes prickle with tears, and I have to blink them away.

Murphy sighs. 'Daizy. Tell me the truth!'

The truth? That's a scary thought. Then again, if anyone would understand, Murphy would. Maybe.

'Everything's just . . . you know . . .' I search around for the right word. Terrible? Nightmarish? Catastrophic?

Murphy is right – ever since I started keeping

secrets and hiding the truth, my life has got more and more muddled. Pretending that nothing was going on did not make my troubles go away – it just made everything worse.

'It's a long story . . .' I begin.

But that's as far as I get, because right about then a plump guy with a camera and a notebook appears at the poolside. 'Daizy!' my mum calls. 'Daizy! Murphy! Over here a moment!'

'We'll talk later, right?' Murphy tells me.

'Promise,' I nod, dredging up a grin.

'What a shame you were delayed,' Mum is saying to the camera guy. 'The sponsored swim is over now, but it was a great success. I believe the children swam as far as Basingstoke . . .'

I blink. The photographer from the *Evening News* – at last!

'My daughter was there, and so was this young man,' Mum is saying. 'They can tell you all about it!'

I remember what Miss Moon said, earlier, about getting publicity. It would be great for the school – and it might encourage people to make donations for the play park. Maybe it's not too late for that, after all?

If I talk to the photographer, Miss Moon will be really, really pleased. Maybe pleased enough to make me Star of the Week! Well, me and Murphy, maybe.

'OK, kids,' the photographer says. 'I believe your school swam 7.1 kilometres, and everyone took part, is that right?'

I bite my lip. Even Murphy looks shifty.

'Daizy didn't,' he admits. 'She twisted her ankle yesterday, so she couldn't swim. It's such a shame, because this whole idea was hers in the first place. The design for the play park was Daizy's too . . .'

'So . . . you're the mastermind behind it all?' the photographer asks. 'Can you tell me something about your ideas?'

'Well,' I mumble. 'It started off with a

shipwreck, and pirates, which came from one of my nightmares. Not the one with the octopus, obviously, because that was the one that caused all the trouble with the Baby Dolphins, along with the stripy socks. Or the iceberg one, because that probably came from watching *Titanic*. Another one. Murphy helped me design it, and then we had to raise money, and Yasmin suggested a sponsored walk, but that wasn't really watery enough, so I thought of this.'

The photographer is looking a little stunned, and even Murphy has glazed over slightly.

'Yes, well,' the photographer says. 'Good. Now, can we get a picture of you? Pity about your ankle, or we could get one of you in the pool. Let's see . . .'

He scans around and spots Pixie, who is wriggling into her mermaid tail for perhaps the hundred and third time today.

'Perfect!' the photographer announces. 'Get that tail over here!'

I'm not sure about this at all, but the

photographer says that a mermaid's tail will
give just the right kind of feel to the picture.
'I can see the headline now,' he says as I shimmy
into the padded fish-tail. ' "Stella Street Primary
Makes a Splash!" It could go on the centre
spread! Now, where shall we sit you?'

His eyes light up. He gets me to shuffle over to
the shallow end of the pool, which is not easy
when you are wearing a tail, and asks Dad to
bring a foam raft over. My heart starts to thump.

'Not in the water,' I protest. 'My ankle!'

'You won't be in the water,' the photographer
says. 'You'll be sitting on this raft, like a real, live
mermaid.'

'But . . .'

'No buts,' the photographer says. 'It'll be a
great shot!'

Dad helps to lift me down on to the raft,

which lurches scarily as I shift into position. The tip of my tail is trailing in the water, but I daren't move in case it unbalances the raft. I hang on for dear life. Pixie's friends have stopped to stare.

'Come on, Daizy!' Dad grins. 'You can do it!'

I can do it – I can. I just have to stay very still and keep smiling. If I'm not Star of the Week for this, there is no justice in the world.

'Right,' the photographer is saying. 'If you could just tow the raft up that way a little . . .'

The crowds part as Dad pulls the raft out towards the cordoned-off part of the pool. The photographer points his camera at me and takes a couple of shots. 'Too many people in the background,' he grumbles. 'It looks like a kid's party!'

'That's because it is,' Murphy points out.

'I need you to go under the cordon, up into the deep end, where it's quiet,' the photographer says.

'You OK with that, Daizy?' Dad asks.

'I . . .'

'You don't have to, Daizy,' Murphy calls.

'I . . .'

The photographer sighs and lowers his
camera. I can see the centre-spread feature going
down the drain like yesterday's bathwater.
Without this picture, we will be lucky to get a
mention at all, squeezed between the Scout
Jumble Sale and the Women's Institute Tea
Dance.

'You can swim, can't you?' the photographer
asks.

'I . . .'

Everyone is watching me. Pixie's friends, lined
up behind me, gawping. Their parents, behind
them. Mum, Dad, Becca, Spike, Pixie and
Murphy.

'I . . . of course I can!'

'You'll be fine,' Dad says, lifting up the cordon
so that the raft floats gently out into the empty
turquoise water. I am adrift.

'Fantastic!' the photographer is saying. 'Great

shot! Just relax. Smile. Go with the flow.'

I drift further and further into the middle of the pool, past the deep end marker. The camera keeps clicking.

'Almost done! Just one little wave to finish with . . .'

I lift up my hand to wave, and the raft rocks violently, swamping me with water. I shift away from the water-logged side and the raft tilts again, soaking my tail, and then I'm falling, slipping, sliding into the cold blue water, my arms scrabbling for the raft, my legs trapped inside a stupid, sopping wet party costume. I open my

mouth to scream, but water floods my mouth, fills my nose, and it's too late then to do anything else as the weight of the tail pulls me down.

16

My hair tangles around my face like seaweed and my lungs burn like fire. I have to get the mermaid's tail off. I pull at the elastic, wriggle my legs, drag the wet fabric down and kick free. The water's surface, far above me, seems so far away . . .

They say your whole life flashes before you when you are drowning, and I think it's true. I can see the time Becca told me we could fly, back when she was seven and I was three. We crept out of our bedroom window and along the outside window ledge to try it out, and the neighbours saw us and everyone was screaming, and Mum had to call the fire brigade.

I remember when Pixie was born, how she smelt of powder and milk, and her hands opened and closed like tiny pink starfish. I remember my first day at school, when Beth was crying in the playground and I said she could be my friend, and then we met Willow and she told us there was a snake in the girls' toilets, and we were so scared to go in there we almost wet our pants. I remember Murphy moving in down the street the year I was seven, and the time he said I was his favourite thing except for custard doughnuts. Ethan Miller and the worm, Mum singing in the rain the year we went on holiday to Skegness, Dad standing

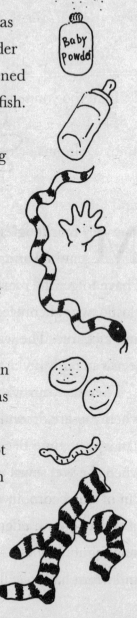

next to the *Haddock*, puzzling over the plans, Miss Moon, Sue's black eye, the stripy-sock disaster . . .

I am too young to die.

I kick my legs, frog-style, the way I learnt at Baby Dolphins before it all went horribly wrong. Strong hands grab me and haul me upwards, and the next thing I know I am lying on the hard tiles at the side of the pool, gasping for breath, pool water trickling from the corner of my mouth.

The world comes back into focus slowly, and a jumble of voices cut through the fuzzy silence.

'I only asked her to wave! How was I to know she'd fall off the bloomin' raft?'

'My wife's a nurse . . . quick, Liv, come through.'

'She's breathing, don't worry. She was only underwater for a few seconds.'

I take breath after breath of warm, dry air, gulping it down, waiting for my heart to stop pounding.

'I thought she could swim?'

'She's only just learnt. She's just finished a course with the Baby Dolphins. She got a badge.'

'Actually, she didn't,' a familiar voice says. 'She dropped out after the first lesson – we never saw her again.'

I open one eye and there is Steve, the instructor from the Baby Dolphins. I should have known. The swimming instructors lurk around in the lifeguards' office, drinking tea and gossiping, just waiting for an emergency so they can sprint out and practise their lifesaving skills. I close my eyes again, fast.

'Daizy? Daizy, can you hear me?'

'Gnghhh.'

'Daizy? Can you sit up?'

Dad hauls me into a sitting position while Mum drapes a towel around my shoulders and checks my pulse. I open my eyes again, wondering if they are brimming with tears or just wet from the pool. I think it's tears.

Dad and the lifeguard are both dripping wet, so I know that they were the ones who jumped in to rescue me. Mum, Becca, Pixie, Murphy, Spike and the photographer guy are gathered around, wide-eyed, and behind them Pixie's friends and their parents crowd in.

Oh, and there's Steve.

'Hello again,' he says. 'Daizy Star, isn't it? I'd recognize those socks anywhere.'

I look down at my socks, and the bulge of soggy bandage that's gone all squint around my left ankle, and a big tear rolls down my cheek.

The photographer guy is checking through

157

his shots. 'I got a great one of you falling in,' he tells me. 'Action pics always look good in the paper. I don't suppose . . .'

'Not a chance,' Spike growls. 'Lose the photos. Understand?'

The guy just shrugs and says he has an urgent appointment back at the office, and I manage a shaky smile at Spike.

'Daizy, love, you're going to be OK,' Mum says, helping me to my feet. 'You've had a few mouthfuls of water, nothing serious. You just need to get out of those wet things, rest a little bit.'

'We'll leave you to it then,' the lifeguard says. 'Needless to say, non-swimmers should never go anywhere near the deep end. That cordon was there for a reason.'

'She won't do it again,' Mum promises. 'We'll see to that.'

'There's a new Baby Dolphins class starting next week,' Steve chips in. 'If you want to come along . . .'

Dad puts an arm around my shoulder, and somehow that helps. I don't feel quite so stupid, quite so alone.

'We'll let you know,' he says.

Or not.

17

ad drives me home, and I curl up on the
sofa like I used to when I was little and not
feeling well. I try not to think of the swimming
pool, where Mum will be
slicing into the mermaid
cake, putting slices into
shell-patterned bags
as the party winds
up and the kids
get changed and
ready to go home.

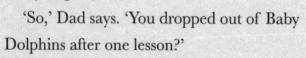

'So,' Dad says. 'You dropped out of Baby
Dolphins after one lesson?'

'I kicked my instructor by mistake,' I confess.

'I thought she was a giant octopus . . .'

Dad blinks. 'Why would you think that?'

'I've been having a lot of nightmares,' I explain. 'Shipwrecks, icebergs, pirates . . . and octopus attacks. I gave her a black eye.'

Dad puts his head in his hands. 'Oops.'

'That's not all,' I blurt. 'I wanted to look grown up, so I stuffed my stripy socks down the front of my swimsuit. By the end of the lesson, one was wrapped around my neck and the other was hanging down like a tail. Everyone was laughing.'

'Oh, Daizy!' Dad struggles to keep a straight face, but dimples appear in his cheeks and his mouth twitches. I try to keep my face stern, but pretty soon I'm grinning too.

'What about the badge to say you'd passed the course?' Dad asks.

'I found it,' I confess. 'Sorry, Dad. I didn't mean to lie, but once I'd started . . . well, it just got out of hand. I've been lying to just about everyone. I had this stupid idea for the sponsored swim, and then I had to lie to Miss Moon as well, and pretend that I'd sprained my ankle to get out of swimming . . .'

'It's not really sprained?' Dad asks, surprised.

'No. It's just bandages and a fake limp.'

Dad sighs. 'That's what happens when you start telling lies. You have to tell more and more, just to keep up, and the lies get bigger and more complicated until they trip you up and you fall flat on your face. Lies are not good.'

'I know that now,' I say. 'Really I do. I guess I'm more ashamed of the lies than anything to do with the stripy socks.'

Dad shakes his head. 'Your mum and I would have understood about the swimming class. So would your friends. And if your Miss Moon is as nice as you say she is, then she'd have understood too.'

'I know,' I say. 'I've learnt my lesson, I promise.'

'It's always best to tell the truth, Daizy,' Dad says. 'Always.'

Well, maybe. It's just that sometimes, telling the truth can hurt people's feelings, or squash their dreams flat. Is telling the truth still the right thing to do, even then?

I think of Dad's dream of jumping off the hamster wheel and sailing around the world. I think of the *Haddock*, a strange, squat, jigsaw of a boat, looming over our back garden and filling my heart with dread, but still, I'm not sure if I can tell Dad how I really feel about it.

Before I can decide, there's a commotion in the hallway. Mum, Pixie and Becca come in, with Spike trailing behind them carrying the soggy mermaid's tail and the newt in a jar.

'Ah,' Dad says. 'And you are . . .?'

'Sebastian,' Spike says politely.

'Sebastian is Becca's new boyfriend,' Mum announces. Dad opens his mouth to protest, then closes it again as he spots Mum's warning look. I breathe a sigh of relief, because that's one more secret I don't have to keep any more.

'It was just the best party EVER . . .' Pixie is

saying. 'Thank you for letting me be a mermaid for the day. Thank you for my tail, Daizy. You are the best sister in the whole, wide world. Anyway, I am glad you didn't drown, and I love my tail, and I definitely, definitely want to be a mermaid when I'm grown up. Will I have to go to university for that?'

Becca rolls her eyes. 'Pixie, you're seven now,' she says briskly. 'It's time you realized there are actually no such things as . . .'

The doorbell peals out loudly, saving Pixie from heartbreak and broken dreams.

'Now what?' Mum says.

It turns out to be Murphy, with Beth and Willow in tow, peeping out from behind a huge bunch of flowers.

My cheeks flare. If my best friends are here, it must mean they care, surely? I'm happy to see them, truly I am. I just wish they weren't right here, in my living room – or what used to be my living room before it was invaded by planks, ropes, canvas and shipping charts. How long

164

until they notice the *Haddock* looming outside the back window, blocking out the light?

Right now, though, they're not even looking.

'Daizy!' Beth says, flinging her arms around me. 'We came as soon as Murphy called us. You poor thing! You could have drowned!'

'We were so mean and nasty to you,' Willow adds. 'We're so, so sorry!'

'It's OK,' I tell them, and they squish down on the sofa, beside me, with Murphy in the middle.

'It's just that you've been acting kind of strangely, lately,' Beth says. 'We've been worried. And we thought that maybe it was because you liked Ethan too!'

'I don't!' I protest. 'I really, really don't!'

'It doesn't matter, anyway,' Willow says, shamefaced. 'We got such a shock when we heard you almost drowned – and we realized that friendship comes first. No boy could ever come between us!'

'Except for me,' Murphy grins.

'You don't count,' Beth and Willow say, jabbing him with their elbows, and everyone laughs and I think that maybe, just maybe, it's going to be all right.

Or maybe not.

Beth sees it first. She looks towards the window and I see her jaw drop, just as Willow picks up the navigation chart from the carpet and Murphy notices the blow-up dinghy Dad

166

has tucked away down the side of the sofa.

'What . . . is . . . THAT?' Beth gawps, and all eyes swivel to follow her gaze. There is a silence, and all eyes swivel back to me.

Dad breaks the silence. 'Haven't you told them, Daizy?' he asks.

I shake my head, pink-cheeked, my eyes brimming with tears

'Told us what?' Willow wants to know. 'Explained what? Just what IS that . . . that thing out there?'

'Thing?' Dad repeats huffily. Pixie just giggles, and Mum hides a smile behind her hand.

'THING is a good description,' Becca says. 'It's the *Haddock*, the so-called boat Dad's building so we can sail around the world.'

'The . . . *Haddock*?' Willow echoes.

'Sail around the world?' Beth says.

Murphy raises an eyebrow. 'Daizy Star, just what exactly is going on?' he demands.

We are in the cabin of the *Haddock*, Beth, Willow,

Murphy and me. We are stretched out on blankets and duvets on the patched-together bunks, sipping orange juice and ice and eating slices of pizza, crisps and butterfly cakes left over from the party.

Mum and Dad took charge, suggesting a last-minute sleepover so I could tell Beth, Willow and Murphy the whole story.

'Can we sleep in the boat?' Murphy had asked, and Dad had beamed with pleasure. Mum brought down quilts and blankets and pillows, Becca unpacked the party food and set it out in the cabin, and Dad plugged my fairy lights into

the extension lead he used for his electric drill.
Everyone said the *Haddock* looked cool. Well,
almost.

'You're crazy,' Beth says. 'Totally, completely
and hopelessly crazy, Daizy Star.'

'I know,' I say.

'Best friends tell each other everything,'
Willow adds. 'You can't just start hiding stuff and
hoping it will go away.'

'We'd have been there for you,' Murphy points
out. 'We could have helped.'

'I know. I've been an idiot.' I look at my
friends, waiting for them to tell me I haven't been
an idiot after all, but they just nod and sigh and
shrug their shoulders.

That's it then. Idiot. Official.

'I lied to you,' I sigh. 'I didn't mean to, but
I lied, and then I had to keep ON lying. About
the swimming lessons, and my ankle . . .
everything, really.'

'Did you lie about not liking Ethan Miller?' Beth wants to know, and I just about choke on my butterfly cake.

'No!' I protest. 'I do not like Ethan, OK? I'm not that crazy!'

'OK,' Beth grins. 'Just checking.'

'Lying was bad news,' I say. 'I couldn't let you come over to the house, in case you saw the sawdust or the maps or –'

'The *Haddock*,' Murphy finishes for me. 'It's kind of hard to miss it, Daizy.'

'I know. I'm sorry,' I tell them. 'You are my best, best friends and I will never lie to you again.'

'Promise?' Willow asks.

'Promise.'

We stretch our hands out, touching our fingertips together under the soft fairy-light glow, to make the shape of a star. It's something Beth, Willow and I have been doing for years – we've never included Murphy in it before, but he's quick to catch on.

'A friendship star,' he says. 'Cool.'

'Friends forever,' Willow says.

'And ever,' Beth echoes. 'And, Daizy, we are here for you, seriously. Even if your sister has turned into a spooky goth-girl with a green-haired boyfriend. Even if you can't swim or rollerblade to save your life. We are your friends, Daizy Star, and we always will be. So what if your dad has flipped and you're going to be stuck

on this weirdo boat for the next few years, dying
of boredom in the middle of the Atlantic Ocean
and keeping a lookout for icebergs and pirates
and sharks . . .?'

'Beth,' Willow says gently. 'I don't know if
that's helping.'

'Isn't it?' Beth says. 'Sorry, Daizy. Sailing
around the world might be OK. You might get to
sit on the deck, sipping pink lemonade as the sun
sets, with dolphins jumping all around . . .'

I frown. 'I'm more likely to be wearing orange waterproofs, hoisting a wet sail. It rains a lot in the Atlantic Ocean.'

'You're going around the world,' Willow says. 'There must be hot places involved!'

'Sure,' I agree. 'Places with tarantula spiders and giant lizards and scorpions and crocodiles. Places with monsoon rains and hurricanes and tidal waves, where they eat raw fish and yak's cheese and sweet-and-sour pigs' trotters . . .'

'You'll be missing loads of school,' Beth says.

'I don't want to miss school!' I argue. 'I don't want to leave you guys, or Miss Moon. I'll be so lonely! I'll miss the tyre swing in the park, and custard doughnuts, and sleepovers, and the Literacy Hour. I might never get to find out what my star quality is!'

'You will, Daizy,' Murphy says kindly.

'Sure you will,' Willow says. 'And we'll miss you too, like mad. We're just trying to make the best of it.'

'I know.'

The trouble is, there isn't really a best.

I do not get to be Star of the Week – it goes to Ethan Miller, who somehow managed to swim more lengths than anyone else in the sponsored swim. I guess Miss Moon thought this was more worthy than making a public spectacle of yourself while wearing a fake mermaid's tail – or maybe word of my shameful near-drowning never actually reached her. I hope not.

There is a report in the newspaper, two

sentences squashed in between the Scout Jumble Sale and the Women's Institute Tea Dance, just as I'd feared. It forgets to mention that we need donations for the play-park project, so there are no fat cheques in the post. We are still hundreds of pounds short of our target.

At this rate, the infant kids will be old and wrinkly before their promised play park ever appears.

I never do go back to Baby Dolphins. Dad says that one-to-one practice is the best way to learn to swim, and now that he is on a gap year, he has time to help me do it.

We go to the pool every day after school. Pretty soon I can swim a width with armbands and a float, and then with just the float. After that, the float disappears and Dad tows me about the pool with a hand under my chin, or gets me to lie back with my head on his palm as if it was a pillow. I can't relax, though. I keep remembering the swimsuit with the darn in it,

or the mermaid's tail, and I panic and go as stiff
as a board and sink like a stone.

'Let go of the fear, Daizy,' Dad says. 'Lean
your head back, and imagine you're as light as
a feather . . . floating on air. Close your eyes,'
he says, his voice soft and soothing. 'Breathe
deeply. Trust me, Daizy, trust me.'

I shut my eyes and try to imagine a glassy,
turquoise sea warmed by a tropical sun. I am in
the Galapagos Islands, a million miles away from
the chlorine-stink of the pool, with giant turtles
and iguanas watching me from a white sandy
beach.

My arms float out to either side and my legs
drift up to the surface of the water like the
points of a star, and for a moment I really
am floating, held up by the water. I can't
even feel Dad's hand beneath
my head.

'That's it, Daizy,' Dad whispers in my ear. 'Lie back. You're on your own . . . you have been for the last minute or so, and you're doing a perfect star float!'

It takes a few more sessions before I can add in the arm and leg movements, but pretty soon I am swimming on my back. It won't be long till I suss those froggy leg movements and start swimming on my front too. I'm getting there.

'Now I really can sail around the world with you,' I tell Dad. He smiles, but the smile looks a little bit sad, somehow.

He's promised to make me a special certificate on the laptop to say I have conquered my fear of water and can swim. I'm going to keep it forever.

That's the day that Dad announces he has changed his mind about sailing around the world.

'I may have been a little bit selfish, trying to make my dream come true,' he says. 'I can see now that sailing around the world was not a dream you shared with me.'

'More of a nightmare,' Becca huffs, but Mum just gets up and hugs Dad very hard, and Pixie asks if that means we can put the swing back up in the garden again. I just grin, because I can't quite believe my ears.

'Doing things for selfish reasons is never a good idea,' Dad tells us. 'All that hassle. We'd have had to rent out the house, Livvi would've had to hand in her notice, you girls would've had to take a year out of school . . . and for what? Just so we could sit under a palm tree drinking pineapple juice on a deserted beach in Koh Samui . . .'

It sounds cool, put like that, but we try not to feel sorry.

'No, if I ever did turn our lives upside down, there'd have to be a better reason,' Dad said firmly.

'Aren't you disappointed?' I ask.

Dad laughs. 'To tell the truth, I'm relieved,' he says. 'Building the *Haddock* was the toughest challenge ever. That boat just wasn't going together the way it should have . . . Perhaps woodwork isn't my strong point?'

'Perhaps not,' Mum agrees politely.

'We'd never have got past Dover in that old crate,' Becca adds. 'Face it, Dad, the thing's a wreck.'

That's what gives me the idea, really.

'Dad, what exactly are you going to do with the *Haddock*?' I ask. 'It can't stay in the garden, can it?'

Dad frowns. 'It might have to. I can't think who else would want it.'

'I can,' I say.

That's how the *Haddock* comes to take centre-stage in the new adventure playground at Stella Street Infants.

It isn't easy getting it there, of course – we have to take down the whole of the back fence. Dad arranges to borrow a tractor and trailer, but even so, it takes half of Silver Street to haul the wretched thing on to it. The *Haddock* is towed slowly along to the school and handed over to a team of council workers.

Dad has tears in his eyes as they attack it with chainsaws. Pretty soon, all that's left is the top

part of the hull, the deck and the cabin – they bury it fifteen centimetres into the ground, then lay springy blue tarmac all around it. They slice a chunk off the mast and arrange the scramble nets, rigging and rope ladder, then paint sharks and stepping stones on the blue stuff. The balance-beam plank and the sandbox go in next, and even Becca turns up to watch as they raise the pirate flag and carry the dressing-up box into the cabin while all the little kids cheer.

'Finally,' she says. 'We can relax. The madness is over.'

Well, maybe. Life returns to normal, or as normal as it can be with Dad still not working. I can breathe again. I still have my best friends, even if Beth and Willow are still obsessed with Ethan Miller. Trust me, I will learn to live with it.

I still have Murphy and custard doughnuts and afternoons down at the tyre swing, and Becca and Pixie and Spike and even Nigel the newt. I can swim now, just about, and I am the proud designer of the new play park, and that's pretty cool. As for Year Six, it's just as good as I knew it would be. I still have Miss Moon, and the whole year stretching out ahead of me to discover my star quality and follow my dreams.

'Sailing around the world wasn't quite the dream I thought it would be,' Dad sighs. 'Still, this gap year is a gift. I'm not going to waste a single moment. What's the point of getting out of the rat race unless you use the time to change the world?'

'Change the world?' I echo.

Mum laughs. 'Oh, Mike, stop winding us all up!'

Dad just raises an eyebrow, and the smile dies on Mum's lips. Becca stops chewing and Pixie's eyes widen in horror, but I'm not worried. Dad's joking, I think. He wouldn't . . . he couldn't hatch another dodgy plan. Not after the sailing around the world disaster. Surely?

There is silence at the table, and my heart
starts up a loud, heavy drumbeat of doom.

'Listen,' Dad says. 'I've got a plan . . .'

DO you want to find out
more about

cathy cassidy
and
Daizy Star?

HEAD OVER TO

cathycassidy.com

watch a video of cathy reading from
SHINE ON, DAIZY STAR

Find out lots more about
Daizy, Willow and Beth

Download Daizy wallpapers and
other cool stuff

Get some fab ideas of ways to spend
time with your best friends

See if cathy cassidy is doing a signing near you

Send in your messages, photos and pictures

Sign up to receive a free email from Cathy every month

Go to cathycassidy.com
now for all this and more!